THE LAST SONG

A SAM PRICHARD MYSTERY

THE LAST SONG

USA TODAY BESTSELLING AUTHOR

The Last Song

Published by: David Archer

"...THE NEXT JACK REACHER!"

1

"Hey, Sexy," Indie said with a sultry voice. "I got the coffee on, and breakfast is cooking. Time to get your lazy butt out of bed."

Sam rolled over and looked up at his wife, amazed, just as he was every morning, at how beautiful she was. "Or you could climb back in," he said. "Breakfast could wait."

Indie leaned over and kissed him, then grabbed his hand and pulled. "Too late for that. Kenzie is already up, and you don't know how to be quiet."

"Me? I'm not the one who makes noise, that's you."

"Yes, but it's your fault. Now get your butt out of that bed, Mister, and come join your family. It's almost nine o'clock, and you got rehearsals at one. Big show tonight, remember?"

She let go of his hand and turned to walk out of the room. Sam threw off the covers and let his feet land on the floor, ran a hand over his face, and got up to walk into the bathroom. He figured he didn't have enough time for a shower and shave, so he splashed some water on his face and headed for the kitchen, still in his pajamas.

"Daddy!" Kenzie yelled. "Mommy's making pancakes!"

"Pancakes," Sam repeated. "Pancakes are one of my favorite ways to have breakfast!"

Kenzie nodded, with a huge smile on her face. "Mine, too," she said. "Especially with syrup!"

Sam took his seat at the table and Indie set a cup of coffee in front of him. He winked at her as he picked it up, and she grinned. "Start on that," she said. "Pancakes will be ready in a moment."

True to her word, Indie put a platter of pancakes on the table only a couple of minutes later, and Sam slid one onto Kenzie's plate. "Butter?" Kenzie nodded, and Sam dropped a big glob of it right in the center of the hot pancake. It began melting instantly, and that process only sped up when he added the syrup that Indie had warmed in a pan of water.

He forked three of the pancakes onto his own plate, then smeared butter all over them and poured on enough syrup to cover them all. Indie was making her own plate, but took the time to smile at him.

"You use so much syrup, it's a wonder you're not diabetic by now," she said.

"I like it that way," he said. "I figured out a long time ago, pancakes are actually a species of fish. You have to give them enough syrup to let them swim around for a minute before you start eating them, that's what makes them happy. The happier they are, the better the taste."

Her face sober, Indie glanced at his plate and then back up to his eyes. "Those must be some pretty happy pancakes, then."

Sam cut off a piece with his fork and shoved it into his mouth. "Oh, indeed they are," he said.

"Daddy, I can't wait to go see my grandmas today," Kenzie said. "Grandma Grace says they're taking me to the park, and then we're going to go shopping for new clothes. I'm outgrowing my old clothes, and I need new ones for school."

Sam nodded, looking at the beautiful little girl that he thought of as his own. Indie had been a single mother when they met, trying to survive by her wits as she raised her daughter, but life had not been good to her. The two of them were living in a car when she answered an ad for someone with computer hacking ability and met Sam. It hadn't taken him long to figure out the situation, and he had offered her the use of the spare bedrooms on the upper floor of his house.

At first, Indie thought he was making the offer in the hope of getting some "special favors" in return, but Sam had quickly disabused her of that idea. A medically retired cop with a bad leg, he had been left with a four-bedroom home when his ex-wife divorced him for working too many long hours and leaving her alone all the time.

His offer was only intended to be for a short time, to give Indie a chance to find a real job and get back on her feet, but the two of them quickly found themselves attracted to each other. Indie, just to express gratitude for the break, volunteered to cook and clean house while she was there, and Sam realized that he enjoyed watching her, and having her and Kenzie around just seemed to make life better. They had fallen for each other within only a couple of weeks, and had been together ever since.

More than a year had passed since then. They had celebrated their first anniversary a few weeks earlier, and it was almost time for Kenzie, who was five, to start kindergarten. She had obviously inherited her mother's intelligence, because she had breezed through preschool like it was nothing, and was already reading and writing at what Sam figured must be at least second-grade level. There was no doubt in his mind that she was going to impress her kindergarten teacher.

"Well, you tell Grandma Grace that your mom and dad want to buy you some new clothes, too, so she can't go too crazy today." He stuffed another forkful of pancakes into his mouth, then swallowed before he spoke again. "I think it's probably time for some new shoes, too, don't you, Mommy?"

Indie nodded, her own mouth full. She swallowed, then said, "I do, but that's normal for Kenzie. Her feet are growing so fast that I wonder if we'll be able to keep shoes on them."

"I got shoes," Kenzie said. "I got lots of shoes."

"Yes, you do, but most of them are too small. We need to take those and give them to Sarah Mitchell," Indie said, referring to one of the twins down the street who were Kenzie's favorite playmates. "Her feet don't grow as fast as yours, they might last her a little while."

Kenzie smiled. "Her mommy and daddy will like that," she said.

They talked a bit more as they finished their breakfast, and then Sam went to take his postponed shower. They had to drive Kenzie over to his mother's place, and Sam always felt a bit of trepidation when they had to go there. Indie's mother lived there as well, and while he liked his mother-in-law, she made him a little bit nervous.

He shaved in the shower to save a few minutes, dried himself off and got dressed for the day. His band, Step Back Once, had a rehearsal scheduled for that afternoon. They were opening for Grammy-winning country singer Travis Bittner's concert at the Performing Arts Center that night, and all of them wanted to make sure they were at their best.

Indie had taken Kenzie up to her room and gotten her dressed, as well as packed for the overnight trip.

Since the band would be playing late, Kenzie would be spending the night with her grandmothers. The little girl was excited about visiting then again, and not only because they tended to take her shopping a lot. The two women loved Kenzie so much that they thought nothing of getting down on the floor and playing with her, or letting her choose what they would have for lunch. Sam often thought that his own mother enjoyed throwing off her daily professional persona and becoming a little girl again, even if only for a little while.

"Okay, everybody buckled up?" Sam asked as they got into their car. Sam thought of the Honda Ridgeline as a truck, but to Indie and Kenzie, it was just the family car.

"I'm buckled," Kenzie said, and her mother followed a moment later with, "Me, too!"

Sam backed out of the driveway and turned toward the main road that ran through their part of Denver. It was normally about a thirty-minute drive to his mother's house, but since it was a Saturday morning there wasn't a whole lot of traffic.

"Maybe it's a good omen," Sam said. "Seems like we're hitting all the lights on the green."

"I think it's got more to do with the fact that there isn't a lot of cross traffic trying to get through," Indie replied. "Most people know that nine o'clock on a Saturday morning is a good time to be sleeping in and taking it easy. Not us, though, we've got to be up moving around already."

"I don't want to sleep in," Kenzie said from the backseat. "I want to go shopping!"

Sam and Indie laughed, and a few minutes later they pulled up in front of Grace's house. They hadn't even gotten out of the car when the front door flew open and the two grandmothers came running out.

"There's a Kenzie!" Kim yelled, as she half ran across the yard. Sam lifted Kenzie down from the back seat and set her on the ground, but her feet only got to stay there for a moment. Kim snatched her up and spun her around, and Grace was already waiting to snatch the child away. The two of them playfully pretended to play tug-of-war with her, and Kenzie laughed with delight.

They followed their mothers into the house and Sam declined a cup of coffee when it was offered. "I'm good," he said. "We just wanted to come in and tell you don't spoil the child too much, today. We'll probably sleep in tomorrow morning, so how about if we all meet up for dinner tomorrow night, and we can pick her up then?"

They agreed on a restaurant, which naturally turned out to be one of Kenzie's favorites, and then Sam and Indie got hugs and said goodbyes. While it was still too early for the rehearsal to begin, Sam had promised to get with Chris Lancaster early, to share his latest song. Chris was the lead guitarist for the band, and while Sam could write lyrics and compose a melody, Chris could do things with that melody that seemed to elevate the song to a whole new level.

From Grace's house, the drive to Chris's place in Arvada took nearly 40 minutes, but once again the traffic was light. They pulled up in front of the small bungalow and parked on the street, and Chris had the door open by the time they got to it.

"Hey, Sam," he said, holding out a hand to shake. Chris slid an arm around Indie's shoulders as Sam shook it, then turned and let them inside. It was a neat little house, which was probably attributable to the presence of Chris's girlfriend, Candy.

Candy, who was also the band's bass player, was in the kitchen pouring coffee for Sam and Indie, and both of them did a double take when they saw her. Candy had been a blonde—most of the time, anyway—for as long as they had known her, but her shoulder-length hair was suddenly looking like a dish of Neapolitan ice cream, with brown on top, platinum blonde in the middle and strawberry pink at the bottom. She set the cups on the table, then threw her arms around both of them. "Hey, guys," she said. "Are you ready for this? Travis Bittner, oh my gosh, I can't believe we're opening for Travis Bittner!"

"Babe, chill," Chris said. "The only thing Travis Bittner has that we don't is a couple of Grammy awards. Other than that, he slides one leg in his jeans at a time, just like me."

Candy gave him a look that suggested he might be an

idiot. "He's also got a major label, a tour bus and several million dollars that seem to have eluded us, so far, not to mention the fact that he's the most popular country star on the charts right now. Forgive me if I get a little excited about getting to meet him!"

The playful argument went on for a few more moments, while the four of them sat at the kitchen table. When it finally ran down, Chris reached over to where a guitar was leaning against the wall and handed it to Sam. "Okay, so let's hear this new lick."

Sam took the guitar and fiddled with its tuning for a moment, then began playing, a quick but simple box pick. He played a short opener, and then began to sing.

I've waited for so long, our good days have come and gone,

We can't keep living life this way,

I was too stoned to see, that your words would never fail me,

But here we are in this place again,

I've been missing out on this thing that we call life,

I finally figured out just what I left behi-i-ind,

How do I get back there, to the place I was before?

How do I get back there, where every door was an open door?

How do I get back there, where dreams can come true?

How do I get back there, where it was only me and

you?

A word that I didn't own to, all of the pain I caused you,
I wish I could wipe your tears away,
I love, and I hurt, and I feel, and I still,
Want you to take me away,
I've been missing out on this thing that we call life,
I finally figured out just what I left behi-i-ind,
How do I get back there, to the place I was before?
How do I get back there, where every door was an open door?
How do I get back there, where dreams can come true?
How do I get back there, where it was only me and you?
I've been missing out on this thing that we call life,
I finally figured out just what I left behi-i-i-i-innnd,

I've been missing out on this thing that we call life,
I finally figured out just what I left behi-i-ind,
How do I get back there, to the place I was before?
How do I get back there, where every door was an open door?
How do I get back there, where dreams can come true?

How do I get back there, where it was only me,

It was only me, it was only me, it was only me and you?

It was only me and you...

Hey, hey,

Oh, oh,

It was only me and you...

When Sam finished, Chris and Candy both had glazed eyes, just staring at him. "Have you guys been fighting or something?" Chris asked.

Indie burst out laughing. "No, of course not," she said.

"No, not a bit," Sam agreed. "That song actually came from a comment I made a couple weeks ago, about how life seems a little dull, lately. Don't get me wrong, I love what we're doing, with the band and all, but —sometimes I just miss all the adventures, y'know?"

"I don't miss you getting yourself shot," Indie said, "or getting dragged off into some mess that could get you killed!"

Sam gave her a sideways grin. "Yeah, I don't miss those parts that much, either. I think I'm getting old, maybe I'm just reminiscing about my old glory days. Anyway, I had said something about how do I get back there, and that sounded like a hook line, so I wrote a song about it. That simple."

"It's a good song, too," Chris said. "I think just about everybody has something in the past that they wish they could get back to, so people will identify with it." He picked up a second guitar that was lying there. "Play that opener, again, I think I got an idea for it."

2

The lights in the auditorium suddenly dimmed, and the audience began to cheer. While the stage was still dark, they could hear the sounds of the band taking their positions, and knew that the opening act was about to begin.

"Ladies and gentlemen," came an announcer's voice over the speakers, "please welcome tonight's opening act, Step Back Once!"

The crowd went wild, because Step Back Once was extremely well known throughout the Denver area. Some of their songs were even played on local radio stations, and every music store within two hundred miles was carrying their CDs. Drums began to sound, and suddenly a guitar reverberated through the place, and then the lights over the stage came on.

Sam Prichard, the former cop and private eye who was now a musical sensation in Denver, was standing at the microphone, and he was halfway through his first song before the applause and the roar died down. As the opening act, it was just a five-song set, so they opened with one of their biggest hits, "I Got Married In The Elvis Room Last Night". It was one of the most popular songs in the entire region, which contributed to the uproar of the crowd.

The next three they did were equally popular, and got them a rousing round of applause and cheers for each one, but then the crowd heard an unfamiliar strain begin, and a moment later, Sam began singing.

"How Do I Get Back There" was an instant hit, and got them a standing ovation from the crowd, which was screaming for one more song. The set was over, and they were taking their instruments and ready to move into the wings when the crowd started screaming even louder.

Travis Bittner walked onto the stage, right up to where Sam was just leaving the microphone. He held up a hand to tell Sam to stop, then stepped up to the mic himself.

"Damn," he said, "these guys are pretty good, aren't they?"

The crowd got so loud that the entire building seemed to vibrate, and Bittner held up his hands to ask them to calm down. When the sound began to die away, he smiled and said, "Y'all want to hear one more song before they leave the stage?"

The response was overwhelming, and Bittner turned

to Sam. “Buddy, I think you better sing another one,” he said, still leaning into the microphone so that the crowd could hear him. “These folks just might get upset if you don't, and then they might not like me at all!” He looked back at the crowd. “Come on, y'all, tell 'em you want another song!”

There was no denying that he was right, not with the crowd screaming the way they were, so Bittner reached out and took hold of Sam's arm, pulling him back up to the microphone. He patted Sam on the shoulder, then stepped aside and began applauding. Sam looked around behind himself and saw that the band were all back in position, so he nodded. He called out, “Everything I Need”, but Bittner held up a hand.

He leaned close to the microphone, looking at Sam. “I heard this one on the radio today, and sent somebody out to get me a copy. You guys mind if I join in?”

The crowd went crazy again, and Bittner waved a hand to someone offstage. A young man came running to him, carrying his own guitar, and he threw the strap over his neck and stepped up beside Sam.

It hadn’t been rehearsed, but it couldn't have gone better. Sam sang through the first verse and Bittner joined in on the chorus, but when the second verse began, Sam stepped back. Bittner took the cue, and obviously he really did know the song, because he took the microphone and sang the second verse perfectly. Sam joined in on the chorus, and then the two of them did the reprise together.

Sam didn't know if the crowd could actually hear the song or not, because they never stopped roaring the whole time, but they seemed to love the impromptu duet. As the final strains died away, Bittner leaned over and said, "I was planning to catch you backstage, because I'd love to record that song. We'll talk later. Don't go away after the show, okay?"

All Sam could do was nod, and then he and the band headed for the wings. Bittner's own band came running out onto the stage, and suddenly they heard the opening licks of his one of his own hits, "A Place In Your Heart".

Bittner's show, of course, was a big hit. Sam and Indie got to watch it from the wings, along with the rest of the band, and they were having a fantastic time. During Bittner's break, he found Sam and the others, and they put together a quick handshake deal for him to record "Everything I Need".

"Okay, you let me join in on your song," he said, just before his break was over. "How about you join in with me on my closer? I'm ending the show with my new release, do you know it?"

Sam's eyes went wide. Bittner's latest song was "The Road I Didn't Follow", Sam's and Indie's new favorite of all his music. "Yes, sir, I sure do," Sam said.

"Good deal," Bittner said. "When I start talking about doing our last song, you just come on out, and I'll introduce you again. Sam Prichard, right?"

Sam nodded, and Bittner hurried back out to the stage. Indie was jumping up and down with excitement, hugging Sam and kissing him, while the band gathered around with their own exclamations of delight and support.

When Bittner said it was time for his final song, Sam did as he was told and walked out onto the stage. The country star glanced over at him, and said, "Hey, this feller was good enough to let me sing along with him a while ago, so I thought it might be nice if he came out and joined in with me, y'all okay with that?"

Sam felt a rush of pride as the crowd roared their approval. Bittner leaned back from the mic and said, "Okay, just like yours, I'll do the first verse, you do the second verse and we'll duet on the last verse and the choruses, okay?"

Sam nodded, and from the standing ovation they got when it was over, he figured he must not have messed it up too badly.

When it was all finished, Bittner invited Sam and the band to join him for a very late dinner, "or a very early breakfast, however you want to look at it," and they happily agreed. There was a restaurant not far away, and they ended up staying until almost four in the morning, just talking and enjoying the company. Bittner set all of their heads to spinning when he said he was taking copies of their latest CD back to his label, in the hope that Step Back Once might get a shot at the big time.

Sam and Indie finally got home at just before five, and fell into bed. Sam wrapped his arm around his wife and held her close, and the two of them were sleeping peacefully within minutes.

Sam was dreaming, and in the dream he was sitting in his living room with Indie by his side. Suddenly, there was pounding on the door, and he leaped to his feet, a gun magically appearing in his hand. As he went toward the door, it suddenly burst open and Grayson Chandler was standing there. Chandler had been the most evil man Sam had ever known, literally trying to bring about the end of the world, and Sam honestly believed that it was only a miracle that he had been stopped. The sight of him coming through Sam's own front door was such a shock that it snapped him awake. He woke to find himself sitting up in his bed, gasping for breath, trying to get the pounding of the door out of his head.

It wouldn't stop, and suddenly Sam realized that it wasn't part of the dream. Someone was actually pounding on his front door, and he could hear his name being called. Indie had also awakened, and was just sitting up beside him as he slid out of bed and pulled his pants on again.

"Sam?" Indie asked, but he shrugged as he walked out of the bedroom. Early in the morning like this, his bad hip always gave him problems, so he was limping.

As he got to the living room, it dawned on him that the voice calling his name was coming from Chris, so he opened the door. Chris pushed past him into the living room and dropped onto Sam's couch.

"Good morning," Sam said ironically, but Chris was rocking back and forth and shaking his head.

"Sam, I need your help," Chris said. "It's Candy, she just called me."

Sam shook his head to try to clear it. "Candy? What's the matter, Chris, what's going on?"

"Candy just called me, she's been arrested for murder! She got up early this morning and went to see her son, Charlie, and I guess she and her ex got into an argument. She says she got pissed off and walked out, but she went back a little while later to try to talk to him again, and the cops were there. Carlos, that's her ex, he's dead—and I guess little Charlie said she's the one that killed him! They arrested her, they say she's going to be charged with murder!"

Indie had come into the room, dressed in the same clothes she had worn the night before. Sam glanced at her, and her eyes were wide. He turned back to Chris.

"Okay, you said she called you. What did she tell you? Did she do it?"

Chris was shaking his head, still rocking back and forth. "No! No, she said he was fine when she left, and she was gone about forty-five minutes. She said she went and got some coffee, and was trying to just calm herself down, then was going back to try to talk to him again. All she wanted was to take Charlie on a trip with us, we're going out to see her folks in California in two weeks. She wanted to take Charlie along to see his grandparents, but Carlos has custody and he just never lets her take him anywhere. Anyway, she said when she got back, there were cops all over the place and they said Carlos had been stabbed with a butcher knife, like ten times or something like that, and they said Charlie told them that she did it. She swears up and down she didn't do any such thing, and I don't know what to think, Sam. Dude, we need your help."

Indie caught Sam's eye. "I'm gonna make coffee," she said, and he nodded at her.

"Okay, give me a minute to think," Sam said. "I'm not even awake yet, just give me a minute." He walked down the hall to the bedroom, and came back a moment later with his cell phone in his hand, then sat down in his recliner. "Do you have any idea who's handling the case?"

Chris shook his head. "I don't know her name, Candy said it's some lady detective."

Sam nodded. "That'd be Karen Parks," he said. He dialed a number from memory and asked for Detective Parks. A moment later, she came on the line.

"I had a feeling I'd be hearing from you," she said as she picked up the phone. "I've got your bass player in my jail, on murder one."

"Yeah, so I heard," Sam said. "Trouble is, I'm hearing that she says she didn't do it."

"And your point is? Sam, they always say they didn't do it. In this case, though, she might as well just give it up, because her own kid says she did."

"He saw his mother stab his father? Actually saw it?" Sam asked.

"Heard it," Karen said. "When she showed up this morning, Daddy sent the kid to his room, but he could hear them fighting. The kid said it got quiet for a few minutes, but then they were fighting again and he heard his daddy screaming. Everything got quiet, so he came out and found his father lying on the kitchen floor in a big pool of blood. There was a butcher knife sticking out of him, a big one, and he'd been stabbed repeatedly. Mama was gone, so the kid called 911, and the mother showed up again about ten minutes after the squads got there. I got called in, and went down to do the preliminary. It's a real mess, Sam, and that poor kid is going to need therapy for years."

"What about physical evidence?" Sam asked. "You got anything tangible to tie her to this killing?"

"CSI is working on it now," Karen said. "There are some bloodied fingerprints on the knife, but they were too blurred for me to tell if they might be hers or not. Looked about the right size, though. Then there's the fact that there's skin under the vic's fingernails, and she's got three long scratches on her arm that match. She says it happened when he grabbed hold of her as she was leaving, but it looks to me like the kind of thing that happens when you're fighting for your life." He heard her sigh. "Sam, I think she did it, but I know you. You've always been loyal to your friends, so you're going to do everything you can to prove she didn't, and we both know it. I'll break the rules for you and let you look through the file, but it'll be sometime tomorrow before I get the CSI report. How about you come by after lunch tomorrow?"

Sam nodded into the phone. "Yeah, thanks," he said. "I'll be there around one."

He hung up the phone and turned to Chris. "That's Karen Parks, in homicide. We're old friends, and she's willing to let me look through the file they're building on Candy, but it'll be tomorrow afternoon. I'll go down and see Candy at the jail in the morning, but there really just isn't a whole lot I can hope to do, today." He ran a hand over his face. "Chris, has there been a lot of bad blood between Candy and her ex? Is it possible he might have driven her to the point she would actually do this?"

Chris made a face and rolled his eyes. "Geez, Sam, no way," he said. "Candy doesn't have any violence in her. She and I get into screaming matches all the time, and she's never even slapped me, not even when I deserved it. There's no way in the world I could believe she would kill somebody, no matter how mad she was."

Sam looked him in the eye for a moment. "Karen says Candy's little boy says he heard it, that he heard them fighting when his father was killed. How are things between her and the kid? Do they get along okay?"

Chris shrugged, his eyes wide. "Yeah, they get along great! She gets him every other weekend, and he comes over to our place, you know that. He's a great kid, I think the world of him. I can't understand why he would say something like this, I really can't."

Sam sat there for a few moments longer, then took Chris's arm and led him into the kitchen. They sat down at the table while the coffee finished brewing, and Indie asked if they wanted some breakfast. Chris shook his head, but Sam smiled.

"Yeah, Babe, I think that would be good. Something light, maybe."

Indie nodded, and a moment later she was breaking eggs into a bowl and adding shredded cheese. Sam got up and got coffee for himself and Chris, then poured a cup for Indie, added sugar and set it on the counter beside where she was cooking. He sat down beside Chris again and looked at his friend.

"Chris, I know Karen pretty well. She wouldn't sound so confident if she wasn't pretty certain of her case, but that doesn't mean she couldn't be wrong. I'm going to do everything I can. If Candy is innocent, I'll find proof of it, but you need to understand that if she's not, there's nothing I can do."

Chris stared into his coffee cup for a moment, then turned around and looked at Sam. "You've got to believe me," he said. "I've been with Candy for over a year now,

I know her. She doesn't have a mean streak in her anywhere, I swear she doesn't. There's no way she would ever seriously hurt anyone. Remember, I told you, she said she walked away and left the house? That's exactly what she does when she gets angry, she turns around and walks away. It drove me nuts, the first few times she did it to me, but then I figured out that if I let her go and get over it, the problem didn't last. We got over it and moved on."

Sam smiled at him. "Then all I gotta do is figure out who really killed the guy," he said.

3

As Sam had said, there was essentially nothing that could be done on a Sunday, so he went to the jail to visit Candy the next morning. Visiting hours started at 10 AM, and because of his license as a private investigator, Sam was allowed to speak with her in an interview room, rather than from behind a sheet of glass. He put his gun into a locker and the jailer buzzed him in.

"Thanks for coming, Sam," Candy said as she was escorted into the interview room. It was obvious that she'd been crying, and Sam gave her a hug before they sat down across from each other at the table.

"Candy, this is a mess," Sam said. "I talked to the homicide detective on the case yesterday, and she seems pretty sure she's got a case. According to her, your own son says you did it. What can you tell me that might help me prove your innocence?"

"Sam, I don't know what to say. I went to see Carlos

yesterday morning, to try to talk him into letting me and Chris take Charlie on vacation, and he just went ballistic on me. He started screaming about me being unreliable, insisting I was using drugs. Sam, I haven't used any kind of drugs in years, I don't even like to take aspirin. Carlos has always been like this, he's always trying to keep Charlie away from me, but my folks haven't seen Charlie in over five years, now. All I wanted to do was take him on vacation to visit my family."

"Yeah, Chris told me that. So, you and Carlos got into a fight about it? Give me the details."

"It was pretty stupid," Candy said. "I got there, and Carlos opened the door and let me come inside, even gave me a cup of coffee. He told Charlie to go to his room so we could talk, and we sat down at the table. He already knew what I wanted, we talked about it before, so I told him I had just come by to see if he was willing to let Charlie go. He started in talking about me not having a reliable job because I'm in the band, and how he doesn't like Chris. I told him Chris is a good guy, and I make more money in the band than he does on his job, so I think my job is pretty reliable, right? Anyway, he told me there was no way in hell he was going to let me take Charlie out of the state, not even for a day, and that's when we started yelling at each other. I told him he was a selfish jackass who just wanted to keep Charlie and me both under his thumb, and he called me a few names that were a lot nastier than that. I told him to go screw himself and got up to leave, and he grabbed hold of my arm and asked me where I thought I was going. I told him I needed to go calm down before I could try to talk any sense through his thick head, and I yanked my arm away and stormed out the door. I drove over to my favorite coffee shop, Sammy's over on Québec, and got me a cup, then just sat in my car with it for a couple of minutes. When I finally felt like my temper was under control, I went back, and that's when I saw police cars all over the place. I jumped out and started yelling about what was going on, because I thought maybe Charlie got hurt or something, but the cops wouldn't let me go inside. They told me Carlos had been stabbed, and they were waiting for the coroner because he was dead."

"Was the detective there yet?" Sam asked.

Candy shook her head. "No, she got there about five minutes later. She went inside for a few minutes, then came out and talked to Charlie. They had him in one of the cars, but they wouldn't let me talk to him. After she talked to Charlie, she came over to me and asked me for my side of the story. I asked her what she meant, and that's when she told me that Charlie said I killed his father. Sam, I was in shock. I couldn't believe Charlie would say something like that because it wasn't true. I asked them to let me talk to Charlie, but they wouldn't. I could see him, sitting in the back of a squad car, and he kept looking at me like he wanted to talk to me, but they wouldn't let me go to him." Candy wiped at her eyes. "Sam, he was crying, it was breaking my heart, but they wouldn't let me go near him."

Sam nodded sympathetically. "Go on," he said.

She wiped at her eyes again. "Anyway, I told that detective exactly what I just told you, and she asked me if I could prove that I was at the coffee shop. I told her that I got a cup at the drive-through window, so the girl that was there would probably remember me—this hair, you know? She walked away and made some phone calls, but then she came back about five minutes later and told me I was under arrest for murder. I guess the barista said she didn't remember seeing me, and I paid in cash so I hadn't even gotten a receipt. At least that would have shown what time I bought the coffee, you know?"

Sam sat there and looked at her for a moment, then said, "Candy, Charlie apparently said that he heard you and his dad fighting, but that it got quiet for a few minutes and then started up again. He said he heard his dad screaming, and then a little bit later he came out of his room and found his father dead in the floor. Was there anyone else at the house? Anyone else who might have stabbed Carlos?"

Candy shook her head again. "Not when I was there, or at least, not that I saw. The only thing I can figure is that somebody might have been hiding in the house, or else someone came in right after I left."

Sam nodded, chewing on his cheek as he thought about what he was hearing. "Do you know of anyone who might want Carlos dead?"

"Ha! Just about anyone who ever knew him. Carlos is

one of those people that just rubs everyone the wrong way. He always thinks he knows everything and that everyone else should just take his word as gospel. Especially when it comes to women; Carlos was the kind of guy who could get any woman to do just about anything he wanted, but it would always blow up in her face eventually. Then the poor girl would figure out she was being used, and end up hating him." She leaned back just a bit and seemed to think about it for a moment. "Look, I don't know who he runs with, not anymore. What I do know is that Carlos seemed to be making a lot more money, somehow, than he was likely to make on his regular job. I mean, he drives a delivery truck, delivers stuff for some lumberyard, but he's got a brand-new Jaguar, a new Harley and he just had a pool put in. You ever known any delivery drivers who could afford things like that?"

Sam's eyebrows went up just a bit. "Okay, you got my spider sense tingling. Any idea who can tell me more about his financial situation?"

She made a sarcastic face and shook her head. "In case you hadn't caught it, me and Carlos weren't on the best of terms. He was one of those guys who doesn't care who he hurts, or how bad, as long as he gets what he wants. Well, that's how he got custody of Charlie. He knew that me and Charlie were living in a motel room, and that I didn't have any money. Look, I'm not proud of it, but I turned a few tricks back then in order to put food on the table, and somehow, Carlos found out. He set me up to get busted, then used that against me in a custody hearing. Between a prostitution rap and not having a permanent address, the judge decided Charlie would be better off with his dad. I'm supposed to get him every other weekend, but Carlos always finds—found lots of excuses to keep me from getting him when I was supposed to."

Sam gave her a sympathetic look. "Tell me about Charlie. What's your relationship with your son like?"

Candy leaned forward again, propping her elbow on the table and resting her chin on her fist. "It's been rough," she said. "Like I said, there were a lot of times when Carlos would screw me out of my visitation, but he always told Charlie it was my fault, like I just didn't want to come get him or something. Charlie would feel hurt, so it didn't do me any good to tell him his dad was lying." A tear started down her cheek from her right eye. "I'll admit it hasn't been great between us, but underneath it all you could tell that we still love each other. I think he knows I love him, and I can't believe he would think I would do something like this. That shocks me more than getting arrested does."

"Candy," Sam said. "You've got to give me something to work with, here. As it stands right now, even though no one actually saw you shove a knife into your ex-husband's chest, there's no doubt in my mind that they can come up with circumstantial evidence. Enough of that to go along with Charlie's statement, and you will almost certainly be convicted. Now, I'm going to be perfectly honest with you. At this moment, I don't know whether I believe you or not. If someone had asked me last week if I thought you were capable of murder, I almost certainly would've said no, but I've seen some of the nicest people in the world fly into a rage, especially when kids are concerned. When that happens, all bets are off. From everything I've heard so far, it sounds possible that you might have gotten so angry that you grabbed the first thing you could get your hands on and lashed out at your ex. I'm not saying that's what happened, I'm saying that nothing I'm seeing so far would convince me, or a jury, otherwise."

"But, Sam..." Candy began, before Sam cut her off.

"Hold on, I'm not done. Just because I said I'm not sure what to believe at this moment doesn't mean I'm not going to do everything I can to find proof that you're telling the truth. I just want you to understand this: if I come upon proof that you're guilty instead, I am required by law to turn that evidence over to the police. Now, is there anything else you want to tell me before I walk out of here?"

The look on Candy's face was one of shocked bitterness, but she forced herself to remain in control. "I didn't do this, Sam," she said. "When I get angry, I don't lash out; I walk away, I always have. That's what I did this time, too, because I didn't want Charlie to hear the things Carlos and I were saying to each other. There was a lot of name-calling, and Carlos was threatening to go back to court and try to claim that Chris would be a bad influence on Charlie. That would put me in the position of having to choose between my son and the man I love, and I didn't want to go through that. I told Carlos I was going to leave, and that I would come back when I calmed down, and he grabbed me by the arm and told me I wasn't going anywhere. I yanked my arm out of his hand so hard that his fingernails scratched me, but I didn't even notice that until that detective asked me about it." She suddenly put both hands over her face. "If that stupid barista would've remembered me, I wouldn't be in this mess. You'd think I'd be somebody hard to forget, wouldn't you? Looking like this, I mean?"

Sam looked at Candy's Neapolitan hair, and found himself agreeing. Hair like that wouldn't be easy to forget, so if Candy was telling the truth, then it was actually strange that the barista claimed not to have seen her. "Funny thing is, that's the most sensible thing you've said yet." He took out his phone and snapped a picture of her. "Okay, I'm going to get out of here and get on this. Have you got a lawyer yet?"

Candy nodded her head. "Yeah, Chris got me one. Guy named Falls, he's supposed to be pretty good. He's coming to see me this afternoon, so we can start figuring out how this is going to go. Sam, I do understand what you're saying, I know this looks bad, but I really didn't do it. I really need your help here, Sam."

Sam smiled at her. "And I'm going to do my best to give it to you. Just hang in there, don't let this place get you down. If I can find evidence to back up your story, you'll be out of here and back with your son pretty soon."

They stood, and Sam gave her one more hug before he left. The jailer came in to take her back to her cell as Sam was starting down the hallway, and he got the impression that Candy wasn't well liked in the jail. The jailer seemed stiff, and the hand he put on her arm looked like it was holding on awfully tight.

Sam retrieved his gun from the locker, then went outside, climbed into his Corvette and headed toward Karen Parks' office downtown. He was early, so he pulled into a small diner and went inside to order lunch. Once the waitress had taken his order, he took out his phone and called Indie.

"Hey, Babe," he said. "I got done with Candy, and I'm grabbing a quick bite of lunch before I go to see Karen. How's your day going?"

"I've actually been productive," she said. "Right after you left this morning, I decided to put Herman to work and see if he could come up with anything that might help you. I fed him all the information I could come up with on Candy's ex-husband, and got something you might be interested in. Carlos McAlester–incidentally, he was named after Carlos Santana, I guess his parents were fans or something–has probably got the cleanest record I've ever seen anywhere. I mean, as in this guy never even had a parking ticket. I've never seen anybody with a record this clean, and it makes me wonder how he managed to accomplish it in this day and age. How in the world can anybody manage to reach his mid-30s without ever having even a traffic ticket?"

"Well, it happens," Sam said, "but if any of what Candy told me about him is true, then it really is hard to believe. According to her, Carlos was the kind of guy who always got his way, no matter who he had to hurt to do it. Guy like that usually runs afoul of some aspect of the law, sooner or later. I guess it's possible he could avoid it this long, but I'd have trouble believing it."

"Yeah, that's exactly what I'm saying. The only other thing I got on him was that he has an awful lot of money stashed away in the bank, and I'm talking middle six figures. I can't find any kind of investment accounts for him, and his job only pays him about thirty grand a year, so it's hard to figure where that money might've come from. You'd think that alone would have gotten him some kind of scrutiny, at least from the IRS."

Sam scowled. "Yeah, it does seem that way. Candy mentioned that he seemed to be making a lot of money somehow, something not connected to his job. Is there any way Herman can find out the source of any of that money?"

"I've got him working on it, but that's not easy. From his bank records, it looks like most of it was deposited in chunks of cash, probably in small enough amounts to keep from having to report anything on it."

"Well, it's something to think about. Big amounts of

money like that, even if it accrued over time, could conceivably be connected to a motive for murder." They talked for a few more minutes, and then ended the call as Sam's lunch was set in front of him.

4

Detective Parks was busy when Sam arrived, and he had to sit and wait for about ten minutes before she came out to get him. "Sorry about that, Sam," she said. "I was in a department meeting, we've got eight separate homicide cases working right at the moment. This one isn't really considered a high-priority case, but that's mostly because the higher-ups figure it's already solved. I got the preliminary crime scene report this morning, though, so I can show it to you. Come on back."

Sam followed her to her office, where she shut the door behind them. "I know you know this, but I'm not supposed to be letting you see these files. This stays between us, right?"

"Absolutely," Sam said. "I'm just looking for a lead, anything I can find. By the way, I wanted to ask you a question. You got a look at Candy's hair, right?"

Karen made a derisive snort. "Yeah, I sure did. I

thought you guys were a country band, she looks more like punk rock."

Sam couldn't help himself; he smiled. "Yeah, I was a little taken aback when I first saw it myself, a couple days ago. The thing is, Candy mentioned that she was surprised the girl at the coffee shop didn't remember seeing her, and that struck me as odd. Most people, if they're lying about something, won't want to point out an obvious flaw in their own story. If she really went to the coffee shop, that hair should've stuck in somebody's mind. The fact that the girl in the window claims not to remember could mean she was never there, or it could mean she's deliberately hiding the fact that she did see Candy."

Karen looked doubtful. "Sam, why on earth would a barista who isn't even connected to anyone in this case want to lie about that?"

He shrugged his shoulders. "I don't have the slightest idea," he said, "but why would your suspect point out the very reason that she'd almost certainly be remembered, casting even more doubt on her story? That's out of character for anybody in this position, don't you think?"

"Could just be she's pretty smart, and figures tossing that tidbit out there is a way to get you on her side. Ever think of that?"

"Of course I did," Sam said. "The difference is, I know Candy pretty well, and while she's a genius on bass guitar, she is unfortunately not the brightest bulb in the pack in anything connected to the brain department. Whatever's in her mind tends to fall right out of her mouth, even if it gets her into trouble."

Karen smiled smugly and waved a hand in the air. "Well, there you go," she said. "That's exactly what she's done in this situation, she opened her mouth and tossed out another reason to believe she was never at that coffee shop. Now, you want to see these files are not?"

Sam grinned and reached for the folder she was offering. He opened it up to find dozens of photographs and a concise description of the crime scene, including specific notes on every item that might have been remotely connected to the murder. He began reading the report, occasionally glancing at one of the numbered photographs. He skimmed through it until he came to the part about the body.

The victim appears to have suffered multiple stab wounds to the chest and abdomen. A common butcher knife was still present in one of the wounds, and was extracted and bagged for laboratory examination. Each of the wounds displayed bleeding patterns that were consistent with wounds inflicted while the victim was standing, before falling onto his back on the floor. Each of the wounds appeared to the examiner to have been made by the same knife that was extracted.

Blood was also observed in and around the mouth of the victim, indicating that one or more of the wounds appears to have punctured a lung. The blood pattern on the face was consistent with aspirated blood, ejected forcefully enough to indicate that the victim was choking or coughing at the time.

Sam skimmed through more of the report, but nothing jumped out at him. Carlos had fallen on his back and had apparently died quickly, because the amount of blood on the floor was not great. Had he been alive for more than a few seconds, the wounds would have bled more profusely and there would have been a larger pool of blood surrounding the body.

When he finished reading the report, Sam skimmed through the photos. He had seen homicide scenes in the past, so he understood the things he was seeing, but something about the way Carlos was positioned was bothering him. He had fallen onto his back on the living room floor, but he wasn't lying there with his arms and legs splayed randomly, as Sam would have expected. His legs were together, and his arms were lying at his side. To Sam, this indicated that he hadn't struggled as he died.

"You got any idea why he's just laying there as if he was resting? It doesn't look like he even tried to catch himself as he fell, and that should be instinctive. He's just lying flat on his back, almost like he's standing at attention horizontally."

Karen shrugged. "It turns out one of the stabbings basically cut his heart almost in half, so there wasn't a lot of blood getting to his brain. Between that and shock, it's possible he just blacked out and fell backward. That's what the coroner says, anyway."

Sam shook his head. "I've seen people fall back after a bullet to the brain, and the muscles in the arms and legs still contract, or something. I've never seen anybody die like this, just perfectly laid out this way. It may mean nothing, but it looks odd to me."

"Okay, I'll give you that, it does look odd. Still doesn't change the fact that the only one we know of who could possibly have been there to do it was the guy's ex-wife. Come on, Sam, you're going to have to do a little serious digging if you're going to find anything to corroborate her story. You can't expect to find anything to prove her innocence in the crime scene report."

Sam flipped through the rest of the photos and then closed the file and passed it back. "I suppose it could be nothing," he said, "but it bothers me. Just curious, here, but did you see anything at the scene that didn't seem right to you? Other than a dead man, I mean?"

Karen sat there for a long moment without saying a word, then looked down at the top of her desk. "Okay, there was one thing that really surprised me. When I interviewed the kid, Charlie, he didn't seem nearly as upset about his father being dead as he did about admitting that he heard his parents fighting. It wasn't like he was trying to hide anything, and when he told me that he thought his mom did it, he said it very matter-of-factly. It was just that—I could tell it bothered him more to say that he thought his mom killed his dad than it did to discuss the fact that his dad was dead."

Sam looked at her for a moment, chewing his cheek as he did so. "Karen, I'm just wondering, but have you considered the possibility that the boy might've done it?"

"Of course I have," she said. "Trouble with that is that the coroner says whoever did it was taller than five foot four. The kid only stands four foot ten, he's pretty small. According to the medical examiner who went over the body, Charlie could not have stabbed his father at some of the angles that were apparent. His mother, on the other hand, stands five foot six, so that fits."

Sam nodded thoughtfully. "Any idea where they placed the kid?"

"Oh, yeah, family services tracked down his dad's parents. He's staying with Grandma and Grandpa, right now." She wrote down an address on a slip of paper and passed it to Sam. "I heard from them this morning, they're planning to get him into counseling right away." She paused, and cocked her head to one side. "You know, there's another odd thing. It was Charlie's grandmother that called me, Carlos's mother, and now that I think about it she didn't seem any more upset about her son being dead than Charlie did. There was a sort of sense that maybe it was just one of those things, something that's unpleasant, but not necessarily that big a deal."

"Maybe Carlos and his parents didn't get along too

well," Sam offered.

"Charlie seemed to think they were pretty close. When the family services woman got there, she asked if he had any family around and he said his grandparents came over almost every other day, and that they were all close. He seemed pretty sure that they would take him in, and they jumped at the chance."

Sam shook his head. "Do you ever remember the good old days, when you and I worked in juvie together? Seems like the world has gone pretty crazy, since then."

Karen smiled. "Nah, it hasn't gone crazy. It's always been that way, you and I were just too young and idealistic to believe it, back then. Now we're getting old, and we have to face up to reality. I'll let you in on a secret: reality sucks, buddy."

Sam laughed, but then he thanked her for her time and the information she'd given him, and headed out to his car. He thought about what to do next, and decided to swing by the coffee shop Candy said she had gone to the morning before.

The place was called Sammy's, and was one of a small chain of coffee shops in the Denver area. This one was on Québec Street. Sam knew it, and had been there himself a few times. The drive to get there took him just over twenty minutes before he pulled up in the parking lot and walked inside.

"Good afternoon, and welcome to Sammy's," said the girl behind the counter. Her nametag said Brittany.

"What can I get for you today?"

"Tell you what, Brittany," Sam said. "Give me a large straight coffee, and could you possibly tell me who would have been working the drive-through window yesterday morning?"

Brittany suddenly looked wary. "Um, I was on drive-through yesterday morning, until about noon." She turned around and started making his coffee.

Sam took out his cell phone and called up the picture he had taken of Candy. When the girl turned back to him with the cup, he held it up in front of her eyes. "You didn't happen to see this girl come through yesterday morning, did you? Probably sometime between ten and eleven?"

The girl glanced for a split second at the picture, then lowered her eyes to the counter. "No, I'm sorry, I didn't. The police called and asked me that yesterday, asked me about whether I'd seen a lady with hair like that. I told them the same thing, I didn't see her." She slid his cup across the counter. "That'll be five twenty-six."

Sam paid for his coffee and thanked the girl, then walked out the door and got into his car. Something about the way she avoided looking at the picture was bothering him, as if it was troubling her to say she hadn't seen Candy the day before. It was possible she was simply feeling stupid for not noticing hair like that, but she'd almost seemed agitated when Sam had first asked who was working the window. The only time he'd ever seen people act like that was back during his Narcotics Division days, when he was questioning a witness who had something to hide, or who had been pressured to lie.

It wasn't likely the barista was involved in the murder, so the only question was who might have any reason to ask her to lie. According to Karen Parks, this girl was in no way connected to either Carlos or Candy, so there would be no reason Sam could imagine for anyone to ask her to forget seeing the Neapolitan hair.

Sam reached into his shirt pocket and pulled out the slip of paper Karen had given him. Charlie's grandparents lived only a few blocks away, so he started the car and headed for their place. The drive took him less than five minutes, and he pulled up in front of a very nice home. There was a Lexus sedan in the driveway, so Sam parked on the street and got out.

The sky was overcast, and Sam's hip was telling him that it was going to rain sometime soon, so he took the cane out from behind the seats. Leaning lightly on it, he walked up to the door and rang the doorbell.

A woman who looked to be in her early fifties answered the door, and Sam smiled. "Mrs. McAlester? My name is Sam Prichard, and I'm a private investigator. I'm working for your former daughter-in-law, who has been accused of murdering your son but says she's innocent. I was wondering if I might speak to Charlie for a moment?"

The woman stood there and stared at him for a good twenty seconds. "My son is dead, Mr. Prichard, and that woman is the one who killed him. Don't you think this family has been through enough already? That little boy had to hide in his room and listen while she killed his father. There is no way on this earth I'm going to let you talk to him, and I would like it very much if you would simply leave." She began pushing the door closed.

"Mrs. McAlester, I've already come across some strange things in this case, and it could very well mean that Charlie's mother is telling the truth. Now, I don't doubt that Charlie believes what he told the police, but I'd really like to ask him if he might've heard anything else, anything that could shed more light on the subject."

Mrs. McAlester stopped and looked at Sam again. "Apparently, you didn't understand me the first time. Charlie has been through all the trauma he needs, right now, and if I let you speak to him you're only going to make it worse. It's not going to happen. Now, please leave, or I will call the police." She slammed the door and Sam heard the deadbolt turn.

Sam shook his head, but turned and walked slowly back toward his car. He could understand the woman's position, but he desperately wanted to find out what else Charlie might have heard or seen that morning. The only problem was how he might accomplish it.

One way was to speak to Karen Parks. It was possible he might convince her to arrange a meeting, but he needed to find at least a few things to lend credibility to Candy's story. Just the fact that the barista didn't want to meet his eyes wouldn't be enough.

He started the car and was just pulling away from the curb when his phone rang. "Hello," he said as he answered.

"Hey, Sam, it's Chris. Listen, Candy just called and said that they're taking her over for arraignment in about twenty minutes. I was just wondering if you had any ideas yet."

Sam sighed into the phone. "Nothing yet, Chris," he said. "I've come across a few things that don't seem to add up, but nothing that's going to sway the cops or the prosecutor. Arraignment just means they're going to officially tell her what she's charged with, and she might get to enter a plea today. She said you got her a lawyer, I hope he's a good one."

"I've used him before, and he got me out of some trouble. He'd better be good, he sure costs enough. I had to give him ten grand as a retainer."

"Yeah, lawyers don't come cheap. If she calls you again when it's over, call me back and let me know what happened."

Chris promised to do so, and they ended the call. Sam drove through the residential streets, trying to figure out what his next step should be. With nothing else to do, he drove over to the neighborhood where Carlos had lived.

5

It wasn't hard to tell which house had been his, because it was still surrounded by police crime scene tape. There was a crime scene van, as well, and Sam recognized Jackie Porter, who was taking fingerprints off of the front storm door, as one of the techs he used to see when he was in homicide. Jackie had been working crime scenes and evidence for as long as Sam had been around the force. She looked different lately, her once-short black hair now long and tied back into a ponytail, but Sam knew it was her by her height; at six foot three, she was one of the few women he knew who were taller than he was. He pulled up in front of the house and climbed out of the car, once again taking the cane with him.

Jackie's partner was somebody new, and he spotted Sam walking toward the van. "Sir, I'm sorry, this is a crime scene. I'm afraid it's off-limits."

Jackie heard him talking and looked up, then smiled when she recognized Sam. She set down the things she was holding in her hand and came toward him down the walkway. "It's okay, Ned," she said. "That's Sam Prichard, one of the best detectives Denver ever had. Sam, baby, how long has it been?" She opened her arms and pulled Sam into a hug.

Sam smiled right back. "I guess it's been about four years, now, ever since I left homicide for narcotics. I see they've still got you training the rookies, right?"

"Of course, that's because I'm the best. Listen, I read the arrest report on the suspect. I gather she was part of your band?"

"Yeah, our bass player. I went down to see her this morning, and she swears up and down she didn't do it. I'm a PI now, although I'd sort of retired from it since I got into the music business. I told her I'd try to find any kind of evidence that might help prove she's telling the truth. Don't suppose you've run across anything I might be interested in, have you?"

Jackie turned and looked at the house for a second, then looked back at Sam. "I can't actually say I have, but if you put on the booties and gloves, I'll take you inside to look around. Who knows, you might spot something the rest of us missed."

Sam grinned. "I don't know that I'd take any bets on that," he said. He sat down in the back end of the van and slipped on the disposable paper shoe covers and the rubber gloves she handed to him. "Okay, lead the way. I promise not to touch anything without your approval."

He followed Jackie up to the front door and inside the house. It was pretty easy to determine where Carlos had died; while there was a fair-sized bloodstain on the carpet, his body had been outlined with red masking tape. He stepped up close and looked down at the spot.

"That's where the victim was lying when they got here," Jackie said. "You can see where his little boy apparently stepped in some of the blood, because when he turned around to get the phone, he left some fading bloodied footprints."

Sam looked where she had pointed, and sure enough, there was the imprint of a child's sneaker at the edge of the big bloodstain, and three or four footprints that got steadily lighter the further they got from where the blood had pooled. The footprints were apparently headed toward the dining room, and Sam carefully stepped around the tape outline to follow them.

He started to go into the dining room, but glanced over his shoulder at Jackie. She smiled and nodded, so he stepped through the doorway. There was a cordless phone sitting in its base on a sideboard, and Sam guessed it was the one Charlie had used to call for help.

He continued looking around the dining room for a few moments but didn't see anything else he thought was interesting. Another doorway on the other side of the room led into the kitchen, and Sam hobbled into it. The room was fairly neat, and there was a block on the counter that held the butcher knives. One of them was missing, and Sam was sure that would have been the one that was taken out of Carlos's chest.

Once again, he looked around the room, but nothing jumped out at him. There was a hallway that ran through the middle of the house, and another door led to it from the kitchen. Sam stepped over to it and looked up and down the hall, then frowned. He turned around and looked at Jackie.

"Jackie, is there anything about this that strikes you as odd?"

The woman wrinkled her brow. "Odd? How do you mean?"

Sam shrugged. "Well, I'm standing here looking into the hallway and staring straight at a back door. I'm having a little trouble figuring out why Carlos didn't try to get out that way. I mean, the murder weapon was a butcher knife, right? If they were arguing in the kitchen, then Candy—assuming she actually did this—would probably have grabbed the knife out of the block there on the counter and turned around to threaten Carlos, the victim. Look where the block of knives is, there on the counter in the corner of the kitchen that's farthest away from either of the doors. In order for her to reach out and grab it, and then even try to stab Carlos with it, he would've had to have been standing somewhere behind her. Why didn't he try going out the back door? Why would he have gone further into the house, into the living room?"

Jackie looked over to where Sam was pointing at the corner of the kitchen, then turned and looked back through the door and the dining room. When she turned back to him, her face had a thoughtful expression. "You know, that really is kind of weird." She glanced over her shoulder toward the door to the hallway, then walked through it and to the back door. That door was secured by a simple deadbolt, but it turned easily when she tried it. "He could've gotten outside, yelled for help. At the very least, she probably wouldn't have tried to chase him out into the yard. So why would he have gone for the living room?"

Jackie came back into the kitchen and knelt down, looking at the floor closely. "Nothing here," she said. "No blood, no apparent scuff marks, like you might see if there'd been a struggle." She got down on her hands and knees and crawled into the dining room. "There's a normal wear pattern on the tiles in here, most of it leading to the living room. You can see a small amount of wear around the table and under it, but the normal traffic pattern would have been from living room through dining room to kitchen, and vice versa." She got up and moved into the living room, pausing at the doorway, where Sam caught up with her.

"The kitchen and dining room are both very neat," he said, "everything in place. Somebody running for his life and screaming might run into things, might grab things and throw them at his attacker. It seems to me there should be some more visible indications that there was an altercation taking place."

Jackie shrugged. "It all depends," she said. "A lot of times, when people know their attackers, they don't actually panic until it's too late. It's like they think they can talk the person out of whatever they're trying to do, so they don't really get scared until the last minute. Still, the little boy said he heard his father screaming." Jackie looked back toward the kitchen for a moment and then motioned to Sam. "Follow me," she said, then turned and went back into the dining room and through another door that led into the hallway. She turned toward the back of the house, where another hall turned off to the right. She followed that one, walked between two doors that were directly across from each other, and opened the second door on the left side of the hall. "This was the kid's room. You step inside here, and I'm going to go to the living room and yell. I want to know how well you can hear me."

Sam nodded and stepped inside, and Jackie pulled the door shut behind him. A moment later, Sam heard the faint sound of Jackie's voice calling his name. He could barely make it out, and would have missed it had he not been expecting it.

He opened the door and called out, "I could just barely hear you."

"Okay," she yelled back. "Let me warn Ned that I'm

going to scream. Let's see if you can hear that from in there."

Sam heard her calling out the front door to her partner, just as he shut the door again. A few seconds later, he heard what sounded almost like a siren going by on the street outside. He opened the door to confirm that what he was hearing was Jackie's scream, and then walked back toward the living room.

"I could hear you, but it was so muffled I wasn't sure if I was hearing a scream or an ambulance going by. That room is just darn near soundproof."

Jackie looked him in the eye and nodded. "Yeah, I'd say it is. I can scream pretty damn loud, and I just gave it all I had." She pulled her notebook out again and looked through it for a moment. "Yeah, I thought I made notes on this. The kid said that he was in his room with the door shut, because his dad made him go in there when his mom showed up. Sam, after what we just learned, I'd have to say it would be pretty hard for him to be sure of anything he heard from inside that room, especially if it was coming from all the way out here in the living room."

Sam nodded, but gave a sigh. "Yeah, but that's not enough to completely discount his story. The prosecutor would come up with some expert to swear that a kid's hearing is better than an adult's."

"True, but that's not what's bothering me the most about this right now. I'm still stuck on your observation, that if somebody pulled a knife on him in the kitchen, it would have made more sense to run out the back door. Now, if the two of them were actually fighting when this happened, I'm having a hard time imagining that he was in the living room while she was in the kitchen grabbing a knife. Domestic squabbles like this, people tend to chase each other from room to room."

Sam nodded his head again. "From what Candy said, Carlos was that sort. She says she told him she was leaving to calm down for a bit and would be back, and he grabbed her by the arm, tried to keep her from getting out the door. She yanked her arm away and got scratched."

Jackie lowered her eyebrows. "They did find traces of skin under the fingernails of his right hand. Which arm got scratched?"

Sam closed his eyes and thought for a moment, then said, "Her left arm, three moderately deep scratches, probably about two or three inches long."

"On the upper arm, or the forearm? And inside or outside?"

"Forearm, about halfway between elbow and wrist. Outside. I could see them clearly while I was talking to her. She had her arms laying on the table for a few minutes, and they were clearly visible." Jackie pursed her lips, and Sam asked, "Okay, what are you thinking?"

"That that doesn't sound like a defensive injury. If someone is being attacked with a knife, they have a tendency to grab at the knife hand with both of their own hands. That often results in scratches, but they should be close to the hand, and because they wrap their own hands around the attacker's wrist, some of the scratches ought to be on the inside." She held out her own left arm. "Can you show me, sort of rake my arm with your fingers like you're trying to scratch me the same way?"

Sam reached out with his right hand and grabbed Jackie's arm, then pulled it slowly back, letting his fingers drag diagonally across the outer part of her forearm. "Sort of like that," he said.

Jackie was nodding again. "Then I'm right, and those aren't defensive injuries. I don't know if she actually left or not, but I'd say she's telling the truth about how she got scratches. It sounds like she was trying to move away from him, and he grabbed her arm to hold onto her. She yanked her arm away, and that's what makes that kind of scratches. She got scratched because he was trying to hold on tightly."

Sam nodded. "Yeah, that's exactly what she says."

Jackie walked over beside the outline of the body and stared down at it. From the position the body had been lying in when the police arrived, it appeared that Carlos had been facing the door into the dining room, at an angle. He would have been standing almost dead center of the living room, facing the dining room door and with his back to the front outer corner of the room.

"Looking at this from a whole new perspective, now,"

she said. "What if your girl really did storm out the door? From the position the body was in, it looks like he was maybe standing at the window, and turned around and took a step or two when someone approached him from behind. If an attacker had come in through the back..."

"Or was already hiding in the house," Sam interjected.

"Or was already hiding in the house, right, and went to the kitchen, grabbed a knife and then came in here... The victim might have heard something, turned around, saw someone he knew and started walking toward them, but then the knife comes out from behind that person's back and stabs directly into his heart. The victim was shocked, the attacker yanks the knife out and plunges it back in several times, and the victim falls back without ever having a chance to fight for his life." She looked back toward the dining room door again, nodded her head once and turned back to Sam. "That's actually a very viable scenario, and could be the way it really happened. Sam, your girl might be telling you the truth. All you gotta do is come up with proof."

Sam rolled his eyes. "Oh, is that all? Heck, I can do that before dinner. Care to point it out to me?"

"If I could, I would," Jackie said. "What I can do is tell you that if I come across anything I think might be of help to you, I'll give you a call and let you have a copy of it."

Sam gave her a lopsided grin. "Wouldn't that get you in trouble?"

"It might, but they can't afford to get rid of me. I'll take my chances. Give me your number, just in case I do run across something."

Sam took out his wallet and handed her his business card. "I appreciate this, Jackie. I was lucky to run into you today."

Jackie looked through the doorway toward the kitchen, and then back to Sam. "I might have been the lucky one. I'm going to rewrite my report so that it presents this theory of what happened. Maybe it will help your bass player, you think?"

"It just might," Sam said, "and believe me, she needs all the help she can get right now."

6

Sam thanked Jackie and Ned for all their help, then started going to the houses close by, looking for anyone who could tell him more about Carlos McAlester. He started with the house next door, on the left, because it appeared there was someone home there. He knocked on the door, and a moment later a woman in her mid-20s opened it and then looked at him questioningly. "Can I help you?"

Sam showed her his ID. "Hi, my name is Sam Prichard, and I'm a private investigator. I'm looking into some matters concerning the death of your neighbor, Carlos McAlester? I was wondering if you knew him, if you could tell me anything about him."

The woman seemed to brighten a little bit, but then her face became subdued. "Oh, sure, by the way my name is Marcy," she said in a rush. "Isn't it terrible, what happened to Carlos? I heard on the radio this morning that they're saying his ex-wife did it. I didn't really know her, I mean, I met her a couple of times when she was over there to pick up the little boy, but that's all. We knew Carlos because he comes—well, he used to come over and have dinner with us every now and then."

Sam smiled. "Then, I take it you knew him fairly well? What kind of a guy was he, can you tell me that?"

"Oh, my goodness, he was just the sweetest thing! He and my husband, Ronnie, they were really good friends, and Carlos was always willing to help out whenever we needed something. He was a whiz when it came to handyman-type stuff, and Ronnie, well, he's got ten thumbs. Whenever we had problems with one of our cars, or something broke around the house, Carlos was always the first one to volunteer to help. Nicest guy in the world, I'm telling you."

"Really? Did you ever know him to have a temper problem? I've been hearing that he had a tendency to lose his temper, maybe even get rough with people now and then."

Marcy's eyes went wide. "Carlos? You got to be kidding, I don't think I've ever seen him get mad at anybody. I remember, there was some guy who came to his house a few months ago, stood on his front walk just screaming and yelling about something or other, and I just thought maybe Carlos could use a witness, you know? I went out and stood just under our carport, so I could see and hear what was going on. Carlos came out to talk to the man and he never so much as raised his voice. In fact, he talked so softly that I couldn't really hear what he was saying, but I could hear the other guy crystal-clear. Probably everybody on the block could hear him. Carlos just talked to him softly for a little while, and finally the guy calmed down and left. One of the things we always liked about Carlos was that he was always so calm and levelheaded. Ronnie, he'd get all upset about something and go over to talk to Carlos for a little while, and then he'd come back acting like everything was just fine."

"Wow, he does sound like a great guy. Were you home yesterday morning, by any chance? From what I understand, Carlos and his ex-wife supposedly got into a big screaming match in his house. Did you hear anything like that?"

"I was home, yeah, but I never heard a thing. I didn't even know she had come over yesterday, not until I saw all the police cars outside. I went out and asked one of the cops what was going on, and all they told me at the time was that Carlos was dead, but then she pulled up a little bit later. I thought maybe they had called her or something, because of Charlie, you know? But even if they had a big fight, we wouldn't have heard anything. That house is about as soundproof as it can possibly be. Carlos, he likes to turn the music up real loud, you know? He did a lot of work to his house, making it pretty much soundproof so he could crank his stereo up as loud as he wanted to go. The only time we ever even knew he was playing music was if somebody went in or out the door, then we'd hear a little bit of it, and then you could tell that it was really loud. Once that door was shut, though, you couldn't hear anything outside, not even if you were standing on the front step." She grinned. "Okay, maybe that was a little bit of an exaggeration, you could probably hear it if you were standing on the front step, but not from over here, or out on the street. You wouldn't hear a thing."

Sam thanked her and walked over to the house on the opposite side of Carlos's place. There, a man in his forties opened the door. "Yeah?"

Sam showed his ID and introduced himself. "I'm trying to learn a little bit about Carlos McAlester, your neighbor who was killed yesterday? Did you know him very well?"

"Well, we weren't the best of friends, but I knew him. Super nice guy, always ready to lend a hand whenever somebody needed something in the neighborhood." He pointed at a house across the street. "See that house over there? An old couple in their nineties lives over there, and you'd see Carlos over there mowing the grass at least a couple times a month in the summer. I know them, and they said he never charged them a penny, just came over one day and asked if he could mow the lawn for them. The old feller, Mr. Howden, he told him he could pay him a little bit, but Carlos wouldn't take it. Said he just wanted to help out, and he knew they were up in years. Super nice guy. Real shame, what happened to him."

"Yeah, a real shame. Listen, did you happen to see his ex-wife come over yesterday morning? I understand they got into a real argument, did you happen to know anything about that?"

The guy gave Sam a sly look. "You ever known a man who didn't get into arguments with his ex-wife? Especially if he has custody of the kid? That woman, every time she came over they'd get into some kind of a fuss or other. I think it was usually about her visitation, I think she wanted to take the kid more often than what the court said. Least ways, that's how I heard it."

"But did you hear any of the argument yesterday? Did you happen to see when she got here, or when she left?"

The man shrugged. "I didn't see her when she first got there, no, but I did see her leave. She came running out the door like her ass was on fire, jumped in her car and roared away. Probably wasn't fifteen minutes later when the cops started showing up, then she came back, maybe twenty minutes after that, acting like she didn't have a clue what was going on. I could tell she was lying, so I'm sure the cops knew it, too. I saw when they shoved her into a squad car and drove her away, and then one of the cops that was still there told me she killed Carlos." He shook his head. "Real shame, he was a super nice guy."

Sam got similar responses from everyone else on the

block, including the elderly couple across the street. It seemed like everyone who knew Carlos thought he was some kind of an angel that was pretending to be human. Sam had expected at least someone to dislike the man, after what Candy had told him. The way she talked, to know Carlos was to hate his guts, but that certainly didn't seem to be the case around his neighborhood.

He was just walking back to his car when his phone rang again. "Hey, Sam, it's me again," Chris said. "She just called me. She said they told her she's charged with first-degree murder, and the prosecutor said he wanted to go for the death penalty, because Charlie was there when it happened."

Sam's eyes went wide in a hurry. "The death penalty? Colorado hasn't executed anybody in forever," he said. "They couldn't even get the death penalty for James Holmes, there's no way they're going to get it in this case."

"Aww, geez, Sam, it doesn't matter if they get the death penalty or not," Chris said. "Sam, if she gets convicted of this murder, she's looking at spending the rest of her life locked up in a women's prison. She said she'd rather they just strap her down and put her to sleep than to spend the next forty or fifty years locked up somewhere."

"Yeah, I guess I can understand how she feels, but tell her not to give up. I've run across a couple of things that lead me to think she's telling the truth, and I've even enlisted a couple of allies. I'm gonna keep digging until I find the evidence we need to get her out of there, so tell her to hang on and don't let depression set in."

Chris laughed. "Yeah, right," he said. "How is she supposed to keep that from happening?"

"I know, Chris," Sam said. "Just let her know that I'm still on this, and I'll come by and see her again tomorrow. Maybe with the things I've learned, she'll be able to give me some other ideas."

Chris sighed. "Okay, man, I'll tell her. Do me a favor, willya, let me know if you come up with anything?"

"Sure will," Sam said. "Keep the faith, Chris."

Sam ended the call as he got into his car, but then the phone rang again. A glance at the caller ID told him that it was Indie calling. "Hey, Babe," he said. "You come up with anything?"

"Not so far," Indie said. "Like I said, cash deposits are hard to trace. There isn't anything in the transaction history to explain them. How about you?"

"Well, I found out that all of Carlos's neighbors think he must've been about the greatest guy who ever lived, which doesn't fit with what Candy says about him. She made it sound like anybody who knew him was a likely suspect in his murder. On the other hand, I happened to run into an old friend of mine from the crime lab at his house, and we noticed a couple of odd things about the whole situation. I'm not sure how much good it will do

Candy, but it's enough to make me think she's telling the truth."

"Good, because there's no way I could believe she's a killer. What kind of odd things?"

Sam started the car and pulled away from the curb as he talked. "Well, it looks to me, and the CSI tech agrees, that whoever killed Carlos either came in through the back door after Candy left, or was hiding somewhere in the house the whole time, somewhere toward the back. Carlos was stabbed in the living room with a butcher knife that was taken from the kitchen, but the way his body was lying suggests that he probably didn't see it coming. It looks like he might have been standing at the window right after Candy left like she said she did, maybe watching her drive away, and then turned away from there and came face-to-face with his killer. It had to have been someone he knew, because it doesn't look like he put up a fight at all. He probably got stabbed the first time without ever expecting a problem. By the time he realized what was happening, he was basically already dead. The knife got him in the heart, and he probably died in less than a minute or so from loss of blood to the brain."

"That's terrible, but it's good for Candy. It gives credibility to her story, right?"

"Yes, and the scratches on her arm match up with her story, too. We kind of role-played it, and the way Carlos's fingernails scratched her arm says he probably did grab her the way she claimed. She yanked her arm away, and got scratched in the process. I found a couple of people who said they saw her come running out of the house and drive away in a hurry, which fits with her story, except that Carlos must have died no more than ten minutes or so after that. Little Charlie came out of his room, saw his dad bleeding on the floor and called 911, so the cops showed up within minutes. By the time Candy got back, the police were all over the place and the neighbors were already being told that he was dead."

"And nobody saw anyone else go in or out of the house, right?"

"Right. Charlie was in his room while his parents were arguing, and came out after he heard his dad scream, he said, but there's something off about that, too. That house is about as soundproof as any place I've ever seen, including the recording studio. I stood in Charlie's room with the door closed while Jackie went into the living room and screamed her head off, and I could just barely hear anything at all. It didn't sound like a person screaming, just like a high-pitched sound, like a siren. I'd like to talk to Charlie and get his story firsthand, but he's living with his grandparents, Carlos's parents, and Grandma isn't about to let me near the kid."

"Well, he's a kid, and look what he's already been through. You can't really blame her."

Sam sighed. "Yeah, I know," he said. "Trouble is, right now he's a kid who found his father dead and thinks his mother killed him. I think it might do the boy a lot of good if he could help prove his mother is innocent." Sam glanced at the clock on the car's stereo and saw that it was after four. "Hey, I'm gonna call Karen and tell her some of this stuff. I should be home in about a half hour."

"Okay, Babe, I'll see you then. Love you!"

"Love you more," Sam said. He ended that call and dialed Detective Parks. "Karen, it's Sam. I happened to stop by Carlos McAlester's neighborhood and ran into Jackie Porter. She let me take a look around inside the scene, and we came up with a couple of things."

"I know, I know," Karen said. "Jackie called me. She says there's a possibility the vic was killed by someone who came in the back way unexpectedly. Sam, there's also the possibility he was killed by little green men who beamed in from the mothership; possibilities are going to make little or no difference from my point of view, or the prosecutor's."

"Yeah, I know that, but it's something else we have to look at."

"Of course we're going to look at it, I already told Jackie to do everything she can to either confirm it or eliminate it as a theory. I checked the report from yesterday, and the first officers on the scene say the back door was closed and locked when they got there, but that doesn't completely rule out this possibility. Somebody might have come in that way and locked the door behind them, then left through another exit after killing the guy."

"Or maybe had a key, and could lock the back door from the outside," Sam added. "I know this isn't the absolute answer, but it definitely allows for the possibility that Candy is telling the truth."

"Yeah, and Jackie says she's probably telling the truth about the scratches on her arm, too. That's all great, and if this ends up going to trial it could even be useful for her defense, but it doesn't do anything to counter the evidence we've got at the moment. Mrs. McAlester was definitely there shortly before the victim was killed, her own son is convinced that she killed her ex-husband, and there's no corroboration of her story that she was gone at the time it happened. Can you honestly tell me that if you were in my position you wouldn't feel pretty sure you had your killer?"

"No," Sam said, "I'd probably be thinking just like you, and if it wasn't for the fact that I know Candy, I might be less inclined to believe my own alternative theories. I'm not asking you to take my word for anything, Karen, but I am asking you to keep an open mind."

He heard her chuckle. "Sam, if there's one thing I've always known, it's that Sam Prichard was the best investigator the Denver PD ever had, and I haven't forgotten how you saved me from sending an innocent man to prison last year. You can count on me keeping an open mind on this case. Just bring me whatever evidence you can find, and if it backs up your friend's story, I'll do all I can to help you prove it."

"Thanks, Karen," Sam said. "That's all I'm asking. I'll be back in touch as soon as I have something more to give you."

7

As a private investigator, Sam could visit a client in jail even outside of regular visiting hours. At eight thirty the following morning, he was waiting in the interview room when Candy was brought in.

One look at the girl's face told him that she wasn't handling her incarceration very well. She had obviously been crying, and didn't look like she'd gotten a lot of sleep the night before. Under the circumstances, Sam could certainly understand, but he smiled brightly when he saw her. Candy threw her arms open and rushed to him for a hug, and he let her cling to him for a couple of minutes, with her weeping as she did so.

When she got herself under control and sat down, Sam began telling her what he had learned the day before. As he talked, he saw a tiny bit of hope begin to return to her eyes. "Now," he said, "this isn't enough to convince the cops or prosecutors that you're innocent, but it definitely shows the possibility that you're telling the truth. In a worst-case scenario, it might be enough to convince a jury that there is reasonable doubt. Don't get me wrong, I'm not giving up, I'm just keeping you posted on what I know so far."

Candy managed a weak smile. "Well, at least you're giving me a little bit of hope that I'm not going to be here forever. Thank you, Sam, I really appreciate it."

"Hey, that's what friends are for, right? I do have some things I need to ask you about, though, so think real hard. When I talked to Carlos's neighbors, it seemed like everybody around there thinks he was one of the greatest guys they'd ever known. Yesterday, though, you made it sound like he didn't have any friends at all. What can you tell me about that?"

Candy shrugged, and shook her head. "Well, I guess I don't really know his neighbors. He bought that house after he and I split up five years ago, so I've only met a couple of them, different times when I've been over there. I didn't know he was so well liked by his neighbors, because back when we were together all the neighbors we had couldn't stand him." She scrunched her face, deep in thought. "I know a few of the guys he worked with, and I can tell you that they didn't think much of him. Talk to Leon Schmidt, or Dean Calloway. You'll get a completely different story, I guarantee it."

Sam nodded, and scribbled a note on a little pad he had brought with him. "Okay, now here's another question. Indie has been crawling all over Carlos in the computers, and she found out that he has a lot of money in the bank, like half a million dollars or so. Any idea where that money might've come from?"

Candy's eyes went wide. "Wow, I knew he had some money from somewhere, but I never dreamed it was that much. As to where he gets it, I don't know. I mean, I know he's done some things in the past, dealing drugs and stuff like that, but I have no idea if he's still into it."

"Carlos was a drug dealer?" Sam asked, looking confused. "From what we found out, he's never been in trouble for anything."

Candy sneered. "Yes, he has, he's been arrested at least three times that I know of. Once for selling drugs, and twice for what they called strong-arm robbery. He's just got friends who make things disappear for him."

"What do you mean, friends who make things disappear? Are you talking about cops?"

"I'm not really sure who they are," Candy said. "I just know that each of the times he got arrested when we were together, the charges got dismissed and disappeared. His record may be clean, but it's because somebody cleaned it for him."

Sam chewed the inside of his cheek for a second as he thought about what she had said. "Candy, do you remember exactly when he was arrested? Or who might have arrested him?"

She closed her eyes and thought about it. "The drug

arrest was six years ago, and it was the sheriff's office who arrested him. He was in jail right here for about three days, and then they just dismissed the charges and let him go. One of the others was a year after that, just before we split up. That time, he got arrested by a detective from Aurora, a guy named Shockley. I remember because he kept trying to get me to go out with him, after me and Carlos split. Of course, he wasn't a detective anymore by then. He got in some kind of trouble, and I'm pretty sure it had something to do with arresting Carlos."

Sam thought for a moment. "Shockley? You mean John Shockley? I know him, but not very well, and I remember he got into some trouble a while back. He got demoted back to uniform, but I can't remember what it was about. He's a detective again now, though." He made another note. "Candy, you mentioned strong-arm robbery. Have you ever actually seen Carlos get violent with anyone?"

"Oh, hell yes," the girl said. "Back when Charlie was just a baby, I worked at Denny's and this guy used to come in and flirt with me all the time. One day, Carlos happened to come in and overheard some of the things he said, and when the guy left to go get in his car, Carlos followed him out and beat him half to death. The cops came out, but even though they loaded the guy into an ambulance and took him to the hospital, he said he didn't want to press charges. Kept saying it was his own fault, so they decided to just let it go. That wasn't the only time, it's just one that sticks in my memory."

Sam looked at her for a moment. "What about you? Did he ever get violent with you?"

Candy shrugged. "He smacked me around a little bit, but it was never anything serious. He'd get mad over me spending money or something, and I'd get slapped or he'd grab me and shake me. Never anything serious."

Sam nodded. "That's good," he said. "What can you tell me about his parents? You know that they have Charlie right now, right?"

"Yeah," Candy said with a grimace. "They're all right, I guess, but we were never close. They always seemed to think I wasn't good enough for their son, so I'm sure they hate my guts now. My lawyer says they already filed for custody of Charlie yesterday, and wanted to file to terminate my parental rights but got told they can't do that unless I'm convicted."

"That sucks," Sam said. "The thing is, I need to talk to Charlie, and they don't want to let me do that. Any idea how I might talk them into it?"

Candy rolled her eyes. "If they have any idea you're trying to help me, they'll never agree to it. If there's one thing those people are good at, it's hating someone. Right now, they think I killed Carlos, so I'm sure they hate my guts with even more of a passion. They're not going to do anything that might help me get out of this."

Sam shook his head. He sat and talked with Candy for a few more minutes, then promised to let her know if he had any news and left.

He turned the Corvette toward Davidson Lumber, where Carlos had worked as a delivery driver. The drive only took about fifteen minutes, and he walked into the office.

A clerk greeted him from behind the counter. "Hi, there, how can I help you today?"

Sam showed the man his ID. "I'm Sam Prichard, a private investigator. I wanted to talk with you about Carlos McAlester, I understand he worked here?"

The clerk, whose nametag said "Bert," suddenly looked nervous. "Yeah, he did," he said. "Really sucks, what happened to him."

"Yeah, it did. Did you know him very well?"

"Better than I wanted to. He wasn't exactly the easiest guy to get along with."

Sam's eyebrows went up a notch. "How's that?"

"Ah, I don't want to speak ill of a dead guy," Bert said. "Let's just say I got tired of complaints from customers over him being late, or having a bad attitude."

"Did that happen pretty often? That he was late, or pissed off a customer?"

"Like I said, I don't want to talk bad about the guy, but it seemed like he was always taking a detour whenever he went out to drop off a load. I mean, we can get anywhere in the city within an hour, but sometimes it would take him two or three. Kinda makes people mad when they're sitting around waiting for materials so they can finish a job."

"Yeah, I guess I can see that. Any idea where he was going on these detours?"

Bert was silent for a moment, purposely avoiding eye contact with Sam. "I, well, I don't know for sure what he was up to. He just always took off and did his own thing for a while, when he was supposed to be taking care of our customers. If it had been up to me, he would have been fired a long time ago."

"I can understand that," Sam said. "Any idea why someone else above you didn't feel that way?"

Bert suddenly looked Sam straight in the eye. "I wouldn't know about that," he said. "You'd have to talk to Mr. Davidson, and he's not in right now."

"Okay," Sam said. "How about Leon Schmidt, or Dean Calloway? Would they be here?"

Bert glanced over his shoulder, and pointed to a door that led out into the yard. "Probably find both of them out there right now, loading the trucks."

Sam smiled. "Thanks, I appreciate it." He walked stiffly to the door and out into the yard, where he saw four men loading items onto two different trucks. One of them was on a forklift, setting bunks of lumber into place, while the other three were loading smaller items by hand.

Sam walked up to the first man he came to. "I'm looking for Dean or Leon," he said, and the guy turned around and smiled at him.

"I'm Dean," he said. "What can I do for you?"

Sam showed his ID again. "My name is Sam Prichard, I'm a private investigator. I'm looking into the death of Carlos McAlester. I understand you knew him pretty well?"

Dean scowled. "Yeah, I knew him," he said. "Bastard got what he deserved, you want my opinion."

Sam nodded. "I had heard you weren't too fond of him. Can I ask why?"

Dean looked at Sam as if he were an idiot. "The guy was an asshole," he said. "One of those people who thinks he's better than everybody else. He'd sit up in his truck and bitch about how we were loading it, but he wouldn't get off his lazy butt to help. And he was always ragging on us, bragging about that fancy car of his, and how he was so much better off than we were."

"I know he had an expensive car," Sam said. "Any idea how he could afford that, working here?"

"Ha! It didn't have anything to do with this job. You want to know what I think, I think he just kept this job because it let him move around the city without being noticed. Who pays attention to a delivery truck, right?"

Sam grinned. "Now, it sounds to me like you might know a little bit more than you're telling me. Any idea why he wanted to go unnoticed?"

Dean shrugged. "I don't know anything for sure, but I've heard rumors. Couple of people I know tell me that he had a habit of convincing people to do things they didn't want to do, or to keep their mouths shut about certain things. One of them was warned not to testify against someone, but I don't know the details."

"You know anybody who might be willing to talk to me about that?"

"I'm afraid not," Dean said. "Just because Carlos is gone doesn't mean there isn't somebody else they'd be afraid of, know what I mean? That was the whole point of him paying them a visit, to keep their mouths shut and do what they were told. He wasn't doing it for himself, he was getting paid. Whoever he was working for probably has somebody else doing the same job already."

"So, what you're telling me is he was a leg breaker? Somebody's muscle? Any idea who we're talking about?"

The guy smiled at him. "Look, man, even if I knew, I wouldn't tell you. I don't need somebody like that coming after me."

Sam nodded. "Okay, I can understand that. Is Leon here?"

Dean pointed at the guy on the forklift. "That's him," he said, "but he probably won't tell you as much as I have. Leon's got a family, he's not going to risk pissing off that kind of people."

Sam looked at him thoughtfully. "Okay, I think I see where you're coming from." He took the card out of his pocket and gave it to Dean. "Listen, I'd appreciate it if you'd give me a call if you happen to remember anything else that might help me."

Dean took the card and glanced at it, then shoved it into his back pocket. "You working for the cops on this? I would've expected one of them to come talk to me, not a private eye."

Sam shook his head. "Did you know Carlos's ex-wife, Candy?"

Dean nodded. "Yeah, I know her pretty well, and I can tell you right now she didn't kill him. Candy doesn't have it in her to ever hurt anyone. If she did, Carlos would've been dead a long time ago, trust me on that. You working for her?"

Sam smiled. "Yeah," he said. "Besides being a private investigator, I'm also the lead singer in the band she plays for."

Dean's eyes went wide and round. "Holy smoke," he said. "Dude, I didn't recognize you! I saw you guys open for Travis Bittner the other night, that was awesome! What was it like, actually getting to sing with him?"

"It was pretty cool," Sam said with a big grin. "He's actually a pretty decent guy. Blew my mind when he asked me to come out and sing that final song with him."

Dean dug the business card out of his pocket and shoved it back at Sam. "Hey, can I get your autograph? My girlfriend thought you were awesome, it'll blow her mind that I actually got to meet you!"

Sam took out a pen and leaned against a post. "Want me to make it out to her?"

"Yeah, would you? Her name is Kathy!"

Sam wrote, *To Kathy, I hear you're a big fan. Thanks so much, Sam Prichard.*

He handed the card back to Dean, who read it and broke into a huge smile. "Oh, dude, she's going to freak out!"

Sam shook his hand and turned around to leave. From what Dean had told him, he had a feeling it wouldn't do him a lot of good to talk to Leon just yet, so he had decided to take a different approach. He had almost made it to the car when his phone rang, and he glanced at the caller ID to see that it was Indie calling.

"Hey..." That was as far as he got.

"Get home," Indie said. "Now!"

Sam's eyes went wide in shock. "Indie? What's wrong?"

"I'll show you when you get here, just hurry. Please, Sam, hurry."

"I'm on the way!" Sam said, and then he cut the call and shoved the phone back into his pocket. He moved as quickly as he could the rest of the way to the car, tossed his cane inside and jumped in. The big 427 roared to life, and his back tires squealed as he left rubber on the asphalt parking lot.

8

Sam hit eighty miles an hour on Sixth Avenue, and was still doing fifty after he fishtailed around the corner onto Federal. He had gotten back up to seventy by the time he passed a squad car, but it was sitting nosed into a parking space, and he was long gone before the officer driving it could get it back onto the street. He knew the cop would know his car, but the tone of Indie's voice had told him not to worry about speeding tickets.

He pulled into his driveway and was out of the car as soon as it stopped moving. He didn't even bother with his cane, just rushing as fast as he could to the front steps, where he grabbed the rail. By the time he got onto the porch, Indie was in the doorway holding it open for him. She had something in her hand, and she gave it to him as soon as he got inside.

Sam looked down at the item she'd handed him, and his heart turned to ice. It was a photograph of Kenzie, playing in their backyard, and someone had drawn crosshairs over her face.

The meaning was clear and obvious. Someone was threatening Sam's family. "Where did this come from?" Sam asked.

"I stepped out to get the mail, and it was in a letter in the mailbox. It was addressed to me, all typed up like it was printed on a computer, but there was no stamp. I opened it and saw that. Turn it over."

Sam turned the picture over, and on the back someone had written, "Forget McAlester." A chill went down Sam's spine, as he remembered Dean telling him that Carlos had worked as an intimidator. Somebody was worried that Sam might learn too much, and was trying to warn him off.

Sam reached out and pulled Indie into a hug. "You know I won't let anything happen to Kenzie, right?"

Indie nodded against his chest. "Sam, when I saw that, it just scared me to death. Kenzie was out back playing with Samson, and I ran out there in a panic. I think I freaked her out a little, but I made her grab the cat and get inside."

Sam looked over to the couch, where Kenzie was holding Samson and watching them closely. The TV was running the Minions movie, but Kenzie had switched her attention to her parents.

Sam took Indie by the hand and led her into the kitchen. "I don't know what I'm up against," he began.

"This case is so weird, with some people claiming Carlos was a saint, and others calling him a devil. I just found out that he was moonlighting for somebody as a leg breaker, a guy who intimidates other people into doing what his boss wants. Maybe that's convincing them not to testify against someone, or forcing them to do something they don't want to do, but I was warned just a half hour ago that somebody else would undoubtedly be taking his place. Apparently, that someone has already been hired."

Indie nodded. "Somebody's afraid you're going to find out about it. But my God, Sam, what kind of person would send a picture like this? Are they really threatening Kenzie, do you think? Or just trying to scare you off?"

Sam shook his head. "I don't know, but we're not going to take any chances. I want you and Kenzie out of here, now, but I don't want to take a chance on someone following you."

"Sam..." Kenzie started to protest, but Sam shot her a look that cut the words off before they could come out of her mouth.

"No, no arguments." He took his phone out of his pocket and scrolled through the contact list, then tapped a name. He listened for a moment as the phone on the other end rang, and then a familiar voice came on the line.

"Sam, boy, it's been too long! How in the hell are

you?"

"Harry, I need your help." It took him about ten minutes to bring Harry Winslow up to speed on what was going on, but the old man who worked for the Department of Homeland Security didn't even hesitate.

"You give me twenty minutes, and I'll have a team there ready to take your family somewhere safe. Get them all packed up and ready, and tell little Kenzie that Uncle Harry says they're going to have a lot of fun!" The line went dead instantly, as it always did when Harry was done speaking.

"I swear, that man does not even know how to say goodbye," Sam said. "You've got twenty minutes to pack clothes, and we're supposed to tell Kenzie that Uncle Harry says you're going to go off and have a lot of fun. I have no idea what he's got in mind, but you'll be with a security team, and that's where I want you right now."

Indie put her elbows on the table and leaned her face into her hands. "God, I thought we were done with things like this. I don't want to be away from you, Sam, and especially when you're dealing with people who would do something like this."

"Indie, we can't take any chances. I don't have a clue who Carlos was working for, or what it is they're afraid I'm going to find out, but we're not going to risk them getting to you or Kenzie. Come on, let's tell Kenzie, and you can get started packing."

Kenzie looked at Sam as if she wasn't sure whether

he was being honest with her or not, but she didn't argue, and only followed her mother up the stairs to pack some clothes for the trip. They were back down in ten minutes with Kenzie's suitcase, and Indie hurried into their own bedroom to pack one for herself.

"I'm not taking a lot of clothes," she said. "I want you to get this thing settled, and settled fast, so I can come home. I don't like this, Sam, not even a little bit."

"Babe, I don't like it either, but I'm not going to take a chance on either of you getting hurt. This is the best solution for right now, and I'll let you know the minute it's safe to come home."

"Yeah, you just better! I mean it, Sam, you get this over with as quick as you can."

Indie was still packing when a van and a car pulled up out front. Sam looked through the curtain and saw George, Harry's chauffeur, with Harry's own limousine. A woman climbed out of the passenger seat in the front and walked up to the door with him, while three men from the van climbed out and started wandering around the yard.

Sam opened the door, and George shook his hand with a smile.

"Sam, it's good to see you again," George said. "Harry gave me a quick rundown on what's happening, and told me to introduce you to this lady, Jennifer Ragan. Jennifer is one of Harry's top security people, now, and the guys in the van work for her. Between them all, you just about got the equivalent of Seal Team Six watching over your family."

Sam shook hands with Jennifer, and invited them inside. "Indie will be out in just a moment, she's just packing the last of her things."

"We're not in a hurry," Jennifer said with a smile. "This will be one of the best assignments we've had in a long time. Did Harry tell you where he's sending us?"

Sam shook his head. "No, he didn't. He just told me to tell our little girl that it was going to be fun."

Jennifer smiled. "I'll say," she said. She looked around to make sure Kenzie wasn't in earshot, then leaned close to Sam and whispered, "We're going to Disney World! Harry's got a plane waiting for us at the airport, right now, with all the smoke and mirrors so that no one will know where we've gotten off to."

Sam's eyes went wide. "Are you serious? Well, that just sucks, I wish I could go."

"Yeah, well, Harry kinda figured you'd feel that way. He said we can stay down there as long as necessary, so if you get done in a hurry with whatever you're doing, hop a plane and come on down. Trust me, none of us will mind spending an extra couple of days so you can enjoy the fun with your family."

Indie came out of the bedroom just then, and Sam introduced her to Jennifer. The two women seemed to click, but Sam wasn't surprised. Harry would have chosen someone he knew Indie would like. There were hurried whispers to explain to Indie where they were headed, and then Sam called their daughter from the kitchen, where she had been playing with Samson.

Kenzie looked up at him solemnly. "Daddy, don't forget to feed Samson," she said.

"Is Samson your kitty cat?" Jennifer asked, and Kenzie nodded. "Well, aren't you bringing him along with us? Uncle Harry said it was okay."

There was another ten-minute delay, as Samson's pet carrier was located and extra cat food was tossed into a bag. Kenzie was delighted that her little friend would get to go along, and Sam was relieved. One of the reasons he had never had a pet before was because he would always forget that it was waiting at home to be fed. Samson would probably live longer, or at least better, since he was going along on the vacation.

There were hugs and kisses, and then George and Jennifer hustled Indie and Kenzie and Samson into the car. Sam met John, Tom and Matt, the three ex-military special forces security guys, and told them how much he appreciated what they were doing.

"No, we should be thanking you," John said. "If we didn't get a break from Harry pretty soon, I think we were all going to go insane and shoot ourselves."

Sam laughed. "Knowing Harry as well as I do, I think I understand what you're saying. Just let me tell you this, though. When it comes down to wanting someone at your back, there is nobody alive I trust more than Harry

Winslow."

John and the others grinned. "You think we don't know that? Any one of us could make three times the money we get now, working as consultants with one of those big security outfits overseas, but you couldn't take us away from Harry permanently with anything less than a nuclear bomb. That old man has saved each of our asses, at one time or another. Believe me, we know exactly what you mean."

A minute later, Sam stood there leaning against his Corvette as his family was driven away. They would be safe, he knew, because anyone Harry trusted, Sam trusted. He waved once more as the limousine turned the corner, then looked up at the sky.

Sam locked up the house and got back into his car, then drove directly to Karen's office. He hadn't bothered to call ahead and she was out when he arrived, so he called her cell phone and arranged to meet her for lunch. "Anywhere you want," he said. "My treat."

"Your treat? Cool, then let's go to Applebee's."

Sam was a couple of minutes later getting to the restaurant than she was, so she already had a booth by the time he got inside. She waved to get his attention, and he pointed her out to the hostess, then went to join her.

"Thanks for coming, Karen," Sam said. "I've got a couple things I wanted to talk to you about, and it might be better to do it here rather than your office, anyway."

"I'm all ears," Karen said. "Especially since you said you're buying. What can I do for you, Sam?"

"I've been digging into Carlos McAlester a bit," he said. "Are you aware that he has a substantial amount of money in the bank, money that can't be accounted for by his employment?"

Karen nodded. "Yeah, I heard about that this morning. From what I can tell, there's no indication of anything illegal, unless maybe the IRS wants to raise a fuss about it. I don't know whether he filed taxes on that money or not, and that's way out of my jurisdiction. If there is an issue, it would have to be with the feds."

"I don't care about that," Sam said. "My problem is that, from the things I'm hearing this morning, that money is his earnings from being paid muscle for somebody around here. According to people who claim to know, Carlos got paid big bucks to convince people to do something other than what they wanted to do, including keep their mouths shut and decline to testify against somebody. What I'm wondering is if you know of cases where a witness suddenly changed his mind. If I can get a lead on who Carlos might have helped out, it's possible I can follow it all the way back to whoever was paying him."

"Hell, I know of several such cases off the top of my head. We had one just a week or so ago, a witness in a manslaughter case who suddenly got amnesia." She thought for a moment. "I don't know, Sam, as far as I can tell none of those cases were connected to each other. I can't see how that might help."

Sam rolled his eyes. "Come on, Karen, think! A guy like Carlos makes hundreds of thousands of dollars as an intimidator, that has to mean that somebody was brokering his services. Somebody is getting in touch with people who get into trouble and offering to make those troubles disappear. That somebody charges an arm and a leg for the service, then pays a wrist and a hand to Carlos, or someone like him. It's an old game, been around forever."

The waitress approached, and they put off their conversation while they placed their orders. As soon as she walked away, Karen looked Sam in the eye.

"So, you're saying somebody around here is running a Thug-for-Hire operation? As much as I hate to admit it, that would make a sick kind of sense. We probably had two-dozen cases go sour on us in the last year or so, when the witness decides he can't remember what it was he saw, after all. It doesn't take a rocket scientist to know somebody's fiddling with us, but we haven't gotten anything solid enough to do any good, not yet anyway. You don't have any idea who might be behind it all?"

"No, not yet," Sam said, shaking his head. "That's why I wanted to talk to you. If I could get a few of those amnesiac witnesses to talk to me, maybe I can find out."

Karen looked at him for a moment. "Sam, this isn't just about your friend in jail anymore, is it? Something else is bothering you, now. What is it?"

Sam reached into his pocket and pulled out the photograph of Kenzie with the crosshairs over her face. He passed it to Karen, and watched her eyes go wide in shock at first, and then narrow in rage. She looked back up at his face.

"Is this what it looks like? Somebody's putting pressure on you?"

"Yeah, it's pretty obvious, isn't it? Now, ask yourself this question: why would anyone want me to drop this investigation, unless Candy is telling the truth and they're afraid I'm going to find out who really killed Carlos?"

Karen looked down at the photo again. "Okay, I'm convinced, but that's because I know you wouldn't rig something like this up yourself. If I go to the prosecutor with it, they're just going to claim that you or someone close to your client did it to cast doubt on her guilt." She raised her eyes back to Sam. "I'll get you the names of a few of those witnesses, but you have to keep my name out of it, for now. Okay?"

"No problem," Sam said. "Now, there's one other thing. I need to talk to Candy's son, Charlie, but his grandparents won't let me near him. Is there any way you can help me out on this?"

Karen thought about it for a couple of seconds. "I can have them bring him in for an interview, and I can ask him the questions you want answers to. You can watch through the window. Will that help?"

Sam sighed. “If it's what I can get, then it will have to do. Can I put a bug in your ear?”

“About what?”

“No, I mean, can I put an ear plug in your ear, so I can talk to you, feed you questions as I think of them?”

“Sure, that's no problem. I'll call his grandparents when I get back to my office and set it up, and let you know when. Any particular time that would be better for you than other times?”

“No, you set it up whenever you can get it, and I'll be there. I've got a feeling that kid may hold more answers than he realizes.”

With that settled, they talked about other things for a while. Sam bragged about Indie and Kenzie, and even Samson, and Karen told Sam how proud she was of her own teenagers. Her husband, Ralph, had also been a police detective, but he'd been killed in the line of duty six years earlier while attempting to arrest a suspect in a murder case. It had actually been Sam who had finally caught the shooter, another reason that Karen was always ready to help him when she could.

They finished their lunch, and Karen went back to her office while Sam went back to the lumberyard to speak with Leon. Unfortunately, Leon was out on deliveries when he arrived, apparently taking over Carlos's role as the driver, and wasn't expected back before they closed. Sam decided he would return in the morning, and headed for Aurora. He knew where the police station was there from having participated in joint investigations, and it only took him a few minutes to track down former detective John Shockley.

"John's in the evidence room, now," the desk sergeant said. "You know where that is?"

"Yep, no problem," Sam said. A moment later, he was walking down a back hallway that led to some of the administrative offices and the evidence room.

Shockley glanced up when he heard the door open, and broke into a big smile. "Holy cow, would you look at this," he said. "I do believe I'm looking at the next big country superstar. Saw you at Travis Bittner's show the other night, you sounded great." He laughed. "Sam Prichard, how long has it been?"

Sam smiled and accepted the hand that Shockley extended to him. "It's been a while, that's for sure. Last time I saw you, John, you had a gold shield. What happened?"

Shockley grimaced and shrugged. "Had a bad arrest a couple years ago," he said. "I brought in a guy on a strong-arm charge, and he was positively identified as the guy who shut down one of the convenience stores out on the loop, but the next day I get a call from the witness who says he was mistaken. I went out to talk to the witness, and the next thing I know I've got IA claiming that I tried to bully the witness into lying. Came down to either taking a demotion or getting shit-canned, so I gave up the shield. You know how it is, Sam, I got a wife and kids. I tried to fight it, but when push came to shove, I couldn't afford to give up the paycheck and benefits."

Sam nodded. "Carlos McAlester, right?"

Shockley raised his eyebrows. "Yeah," he said. "You knew about that?"

"I heard something about it recently," Sam said. "Did you hear that he was killed Sunday morning?"

"Yeah," Shockley said, nodding his head. "News says his ex did it. You working that case?"

"His ex is the bass player in my band, so I dusted off my PI license to see what I can find out."

Shockley's face became cold, all the friendliness drained away. "Sam, are you looking at me as a suspect? I can save you a lot of time, I was working here Sunday morning."

Sam smiled. "Oh, good grief, John, no," Sam said. "I just wanted to know more about your run in with him. Seems Carlos worked as a leg breaker for someone around here, and one of his specialties is to make witnesses change their minds. Did you ever find any indication that he may have been the one to intimidate your witness?"

Shockley frowned, but he had relaxed considerably. "No. In fact, I couldn't ever get him to talk at all. I did hear that it was someone else who got to him, threatened his wife, but I couldn't prove it." He waved a hand to indicate the room around him. "That's why I'm here."

"John, did you ever get anything on who was behind

it? Any clue at all? I'm hoping that if I can find that out, I might find out who really killed him."

"Nothing, not even a hint. If he was doing muscle work, then I'd guess it was whoever pulled his strings. Must have wanted him to stay out on the street."

The two men talked for a few more minutes, but Shockley didn't have anything more to offer, so, with nothing else to do, Sam decided to head for home. It wasn't a long drive, but he had just gotten back into the house and dug a root beer out of the refrigerator when his phone rang. He glanced at the caller ID to see that it was Karen Parks calling.

"Hello," he said.

"Sam, it's Karen. Listen, I called out to the McAlesters' place to arrange that interview, but the grandmother just called me back. She went to find Charlie to tell him they'd be coming down to the station in the morning, and found a note in his bedroom. He's run away, Sam, and the note said he was going to try to find a way to save his mom. They checked all his friends, and nobody knows where he is. Under the circumstances, we're opening a file on it now, and we've got an APB out on him already. I'll let you know if we find anything."

Sam's eyes widened in shock. "Holy cow," he said. "Does it strike you as odd that he would say his mother killed his father, but he wants to save her?"

"Sam, I'm beginning to think odd doesn't come close

to describing this case."

9

Sam's phone rang again about twenty minutes later, and he answered it to hear the familiar recording.

"This call is from," said the recorded voice, and then he heard Candy's voice giving her name before it went on, "an inmate at the Denver County Jail. To accept this call, dial five. To block all future calls from this inmate, dial nine."

Sam punched the five, and heard Candy crying. "Candy, it's Sam," he said.

"Oh, Sam, they just told me that Charlie has disappeared. Sam, please see if you can find him, please? He's all I've got, Sam, and I'm scared to death. What if Carlos is mixed up with bad people, and they've got Charlie now?"

It took Sam several minutes to get her calmed down at all, but he promised to do everything he could to help the police find her son. He had also worried that Charlie might have actually been taken, used as a pawn or some sort of collateral to try to make sure no one got any closer to the truth. So far, there'd been no indication that this was the case, but that didn't keep Sam from worrying.

When he finally got off the phone, Sam tried calling Indie, but her phone went straight to voicemail. He left a message for her to call when she could, just to let him know she was okay, and then sat down in the living room and turned on the TV. At that moment, all he wanted was something to take his mind off of the case he had gotten entangled in.

Sometimes, though, fate has other plans. He had just finished watching an old rerun of *Supernatural* when he heard a car pull up in his driveway. He pushed himself up out of his recliner and went to the door just as someone knocked. He opened the door to find his mother-in-law, Kim, standing there, and she brushed past him into the house.

"Now, Sam, I know you're going to get upset about this," Kim began, "and I promise you I wouldn't bother you if it wasn't important, but..."

"Beauregard?" Sam asked. Beauregard was the name Kim claimed for her "spirit guide," which she insisted was the ghost of a Civil War soldier. Sam wasn't exactly a believer in Beauregard, but he couldn't deny the fact that the warnings Kim gave him from what Sam figured was her own alter ego had helped in his investigations and even saved his life more than once. When Beauregard spoke, Sam had learned that it was usually a good idea to listen.

Kim looked at him for a moment with her lips pressed tightly together. "Yes. He told me to get over here and talk to you right now. Sam, I don't know what you're doing, but Beauregard says you've got to stop worrying about anything except the little boy. He won't tell me any details, but he says the little boy has the answer you need."

Sam shook his head, an exasperated look on his face. "Well, that's just wonderful, Kim, except for the fact that the little boy has run away from home and nobody knows where he is. Can Beauregard help me with that?"

Kim stared at him for a moment, then closed her eyes. He could see her lips moving. A moment passed, and then she opened her eyes and looked at him again. "Beauregard says the little boy will come to you. He doesn't know when, but sometime in the next couple of days you're going to hear from him. When you do, it will be up to you to keep him safe." She looked around the room, and then said, "Where are Kenzie and Indiana?"

Sam groaned. "Um, they went to Disney World. They got a free trip, and had to go today. I'm surprised Indie didn't call you."

Kim stood there for just a moment, then closed her eyes again. When she opened them this time, they were filled with fire. "Sam Prichard! How dare you lie to me!

Why didn't someone call and tell me she'd been threatened?"

"What? Indie hasn't been threatened..."

"No, you idiot, not Indie, I'm talking about McKenzie! Beauregard says you got some kind of a message threatening her if you don't stop investigating whatever you're working on!"

Sam put a hand over his eyes. "Do me a favor, will you, Kim? Tell Beauregard that sooner or later I'm going to find a way to kill him! Look, yes, I got a message like that, and I did exactly what needed to be done. I called Harry Winslow, and he arranged this trip to Disney World. They've got a top security team with them, and they're perfectly safe, now."

The small woman stepped forward until she was chest to belly with Sam, who towered over her. "They had just better be," she said in tones that dripped with anger. Then, without another word, she turned and walked out the door, got into her car and drove away.

Sam stood stock still in the middle of his front doorway for a moment, then slowly closed the door and went back to his chair.

"Beauregard," he said to no one. "This is one time, buddy, I really hope you're right."

Indie called an hour later, and told Sam that they had arrived safely in Orlando. Someone at the hotel had given Jennifer their passes, which included Disney World and Universal Studios, so she was quite certain that Kenzie was about to have the time of her life.

"I miss you already," she said, and Sam told her that he felt the same way. They talked for a couple of minutes, and then Sam told Indie about her mother's visit, and Beauregard's message.

Indie sighed. "Sam, I know you hate it, but that old spook is always right. You know that as well as I do. If he says the boy will get in touch with you, then you might as well just sit around and wait."

"Yeah, I know, that's what burns my ass. I want to be out there doing something, but I don't have any more leads to work, not really. It's like I've come up on a dead end."

"Well, maybe that's because you're thinking like a private investigator. Think like a kid; if you were an eight-year-old boy and wanted to hide, what would you do?"

Sam thought about it. "I'd find a friend who knew how to keep a secret," he said.

"Well, there you go. Is there any way you can find out who his friends are? Or better yet, find out where he goes to school. In fact, give me just a minute, I've already got my computer set up here in the hotel and on the Wi-Fi." Sam heard her tapping on the keys of her laptop, and a moment later she said, "Aha! Charlie goes to Raynor Elementary School, it's a private school on East Alameda. He must be an advanced student, he's in the fifth grade already. His teacher is Becky Martinez. Sam, what you need to do is go and speak to his teacher in the morning. She would probably know who he's close to."

Sam nodded into the phone. "Baby, that's an excellent idea. I'll go first thing tomorrow."

They talked for a few more minutes, and then Sam got to talk to Kenzie, who assured him that Samson was having a wonderful time, as well. Kenzie had taught Samson to walk on a leash when he was only a kitten, which was a pretty good idea since he had some sort of nerve damage that occasionally made his back end pass up his front end, causing him to look like a rolling, furry cannonball whenever he tried to run too quickly. Because of this, he would even get to go along to the parks the next day.

Kenzie finally let her mother have the phone back, and Sam and his wife whispered their affections to each other for a few more minutes, but then it was time for the call to end. Jennifer was in charge of pretty much everything, and it was time for them to go and find some dinner. That reminded Sam that he was getting hungry, himself, and he wandered into the kitchen to dig in the freezer for something he could pop in the microwave.

Two large red-hot burritos and another bottle of root beer later, Sam plopped into his recliner again and watched a movie. Indie called at around nine, and they talked for a few more minutes, then Sam went into his bedroom to get some sleep.

Five minutes later, he carried his pillow out to the

couch. The bed just wasn't going to work, not when Indie wasn't in it with him.

10

Sam walked into Raynor Elementary a few minutes before it opened the next morning and asked to speak to Ms. Martinez. The secretary told him to wait, and a moment later the principal, Mrs. Jackson, came out to ask him what he needed. Sam showed his ID and explained the situation. After a moment of thought, Mrs. Jackson led him to Ms. Martinez's classroom and explained to the teacher that Charlie had apparently run away. Sam, she said, was a private investigator who wanted to speak to the class about whether they had any idea where Charlie would go.

Ms. Martinez said she was happy to help, and when the students finally filed in, she introduced him to them. "Mr. Prichard is what they call a private investigator, like a policeman. He's looking for Charlie McAlester, who seems to be missing." She looked at Sam and nodded encouragingly.

Sam stepped up before the class and looked out over the sea of little faces that were staring at him. "Hi, kids," he began. "Well, like your teacher told you, Charlie has run away, and we're all very worried about him. I know he hasn't been in class the last couple of days, but that was because something bad happened at his house, and we're all afraid that it's got him pretty upset. I wanted to ask if any of you might have some idea of where Charlie might go, someplace he might want to hide. If you do, please let me know, because it's very important that we find him soon."

The kids all looked to one another, but nobody spoke up. "Okay, well listen, if you do happen to hear from him or think of somewhere he might go, I would appreciate it if you would ask your parents to call me as soon as you can, or if they don't want to call me, then they could call the police. I'm going to give each one of you my business card, so you can call me anytime if you know anything about Charlie, or how I might be able to help him." He had brought a stack of business cards with him for this very reason, and Ms. Martinez had two of the children in the front row take them from him and pass them out. Sam thanked the teacher and the children, and then left the school.

Once again, Sam felt like he was at a dead end. The message from Beauregard echoed through his mind, that he should simply wait for Charlie to get in touch with him. He turned the Corvette toward home again, and spent the whole day just hanging around the house.

Indie called him a few times, and he was delighted to hear how much fun they were having. He didn't tell her that he had been so lonely the night before that he slept on the couch. Instead, he told her about talking to the students that morning, and how he was hoping that Beauregard's prediction would come true.

He fielded a couple of calls from the other band members, Janice Peet and Stan Bennett. He assured them both that he was doing everything he could to help Candy, which is what they seemed to want to hear. Each of them was convinced she was innocent, and they were counting on Sam to do the impossible once again. After all, they had met Sam when their original lead singer had disappeared, and they had hired him to find the fellow. Unfortunately, Sam had found him dead, and it was only an accident that led to them finding out Sam could sing.

Chris called, and Candy called, and Sam did everything he could to keep all of their spirits up. He had learned long ago, as a police officer, that it was necessary to keep his own voice sounding confident so that other people wouldn't give up. Looking back, he was glad he had taken that lesson to heart.

Evening finally fell, and Sam continued his boring routine of the day, watching television and drinking more root beer than was probably good for him. He watched a couple more *Supernatural* episodes on Netflix, then found a movie about the war in Afghanistan and started watching that. It was nearly eight o'clock, and he was waiting for Indie to call and let him talk to Kenzie before she went to bed. It was two hours later in Orlando, so the call would be coming anytime.

When the phone rang a moment later, he didn't even look at the caller ID. He picked it up and said, "Hey, gorgeous."

A very young voice that sounded surprised said, "Is this Mr. Prichard?"

Sam's eyes flew wide open. "Yes, it is," he said. "I'm sorry about that, I thought it was my wife calling."

"Oh. Oh, that's okay. My name is Cindy, you came and talked to our class this morning. About Charlie, you said you were looking for him."

"Yes," Sam said. "Yes, I am. Do you know where he might be?"

There was silence on the line for a few seconds, and Sam began to worry that he had scared the little girl off. Finally she spoke. "If I know where he is, and I tell you, is he going to be in trouble?"

"No, not at all. Charlie hasn't done anything wrong, we just need to find him to make sure he's safe."

"But what if he's already safe, and he doesn't want anyone to know where he is? What if he's afraid to go home? Would you have to take him home?"

Sam thought, *Well, this puts a wrinkle into things.* Aloud, he said, "Not necessarily. If there's a reason why he doesn't want to go home, then maybe we can find him somewhere else he could stay, somewhere he'd be safe and comfortable."

Once again there was silence, but it didn't last as long. "Well—he's here at my house, out in our garage, but he's afraid to talk to anybody. I told him I thought it would be okay to talk to you. If I give you our address, would you be willing to come over by yourself and talk to him?"

Sam thought quickly. Under normal circumstances, he wouldn't even consider agreeing to a request like that, but for all he knew Charlie might be in danger. He wanted to know more about why Charlie ran away from his grandparents before he decided whether to report his whereabouts to the police.

"Yes, I could do that. When?"

"Well, maybe, like now? And—and would you bring him something to eat? I tried to sneak some food out to him, but my dad caught me. He doesn't want my dad to know he's here."

Sam smiled. "Sure, I can do that. What's the address?"

Cindy gave him the address and told him that Charlie would be waiting for him in the garage. It opened onto the alley behind the house, so Sam could park a little ways down and get there without being seen. Sam promised to be there within half an hour, and to bring a big box of fried chicken with him.

Because the Corvette was both loud and flashy, Sam decided to take the Honda Ridgeline that he had bought for Indie to drive, instead. The truck was quiet, and nobody seemed to pay a lot of attention to it. He thought it would be a good idea to be as discreet as possible.

Indie called while he was pulling away from the house, and he filled her in on what was going on. She told him how glad she was that Charlie's little friend had reached out to him, and they both avoided mentioning Beauregard's prediction that something like that would happen. She let Kenzie talk to Sam for a couple of minutes, and he heard all about their first day at Disney World. The little girl seemed to have had a blast, and Sam wished once again that he was there to enjoy it with her.

Indie came back on the phone and they talked for a couple more minutes, whispering words of love and how each wished to be with the other. They hung up, with Sam promising to call and let her know how things went with Charlie.

He made a quick stop at the KFC and bought a double three-piece meal, then headed for the address Cindy had given him. He found it easily with his phone's GPS, and turned off his lights as he pulled into the alley. He parked a couple houses down from the garage, walked over, and tapped lightly on the garage door.

A small round face appeared in one of the frames where a window had been broken out. "Charlie?" Sam asked, and the face nodded. The boy held up a finger to tell Sam to wait, and then a smaller door on the side of the building opened with a creak. Charlie came around the building and stood just out of Sam's reach, as if he was ready to run if he had to.

"I got you some chicken," Sam said. He held out the bag, and after a moment the boy took it. Sam stood there for a second, then sat down on the ground and leaned back against the front bumper of the Ridgeline. After a few seconds, Charlie sat down and leaned back against the garage, then tore into the chicken, clearly famished.

"Charlie, I know we haven't met, but I'm a friend of your mother. You know she's in a band, right? Well, I'm the singer."

Charlie looked up at him, with half a chicken leg already in his mouth. He nodded his head, as if telling Sam to go on.

"Charlie, can you tell me why you ran away from your grandparents?"

Charlie ate the rest of the chicken leg and devoured a wing before he answered. He swallowed hard, then said, "I had to get out of there. All they did was talk bad about my mom."

Sam smiled and nodded. "Okay, I guess I can understand that. But, Charlie, they still think your mom killed your dad. It's probably normal for them to be mad at her right now, don't you think?"

"Well, yeah, I could understand that," Charlie said. "It's worse than that, though, they keep saying that she should have been locked away a long time ago, and that she's a bad mother and stuff like that. She's not a bad mother, no matter what she's done."

Charlie ripped into a chicken breast, and Sam let him eat for a couple of minutes before he asked any more questions. When the boy showed signs of slowing down, Sam started talking again. "Charlie, the police said you told them that your mom killed your dad. Do you really believe that's true?"

Charlie sat there and looked down into the box of chicken in his lap for a long moment, then looked up at Sam. "Well, I think she did," he said slowly. "They were fighting and yelling, and then I think I heard my dad screaming like he was hurt. I wasn't supposed to leave my room, but I waited to see if there was going to be any more fighting, then I ran out to see what was going on. He was already lying on the floor, and I guess he was already dead. I didn't know what else to do, so I called 911, like they always tell us to do."

"Charlie," Sam said, "was there anybody else at the house that morning?"

Charlie shook his head. "Uh-uh, not by the time my mom got there. I think my dad's girlfriend was there a little before that, though. Whenever she comes over, Dad made me go in my room. He said I was too young to see him and his girlfriend together, so I always had to go in my room and watch TV there."

"So you didn't see her there?" If Sam could establish that someone else had been in the house that morning, it would be another bit of doubt as to Candy's guilt.

Charlie shook his head once again. "No, I never did see her. Well, just once, but I didn't get to see her face. She and my dad were–you know, doing stuff. It was late at night, and I got up to go to the bathroom and I heard something in the living room. I looked, and they were on the couch but when I saw it was them I hurried up and went back to my room."

"Okay, no problem. Do you know her name?"

"Uh-uh. My dad always just called her Sweetie Pie, that's all I know. But she wasn't there when my mom got there, I know that. I was out of my room then, but Dad made me go back when they started fighting."

Sam sat there on the ground, and wondered what else he might ask. "Charlie, do you know who your dad worked for? Not his job at the lumberyard, but his other job. Do you know?"

More head shaking. "No, but sometimes he would get a phone call, and had to leave all of a sudden. He always said it was work, but I knew it wasn't at the lumberyard. They were closed a lot of times when he got those phone calls."

Sam waited while Charlie started on the second box of chicken, but his appetite seemed to have run down. He managed to eat a wing, but then he closed the box and put it back in the bag.

"Charlie, your mom told me that she left the house to get some coffee and calm down, because she and your dad were fighting. She said he was alive and well when she left, but by the time she got back he was dead. Now, I've been in your house, and even in your bedroom. If you had the door shut, it was probably pretty hard to hear what was going on out in the living room, right?"

Charlie nodded. "Yeah, Dad liked it that way."

"Okay, then, do you think it's possible that your mom left like she said, and that somebody else might have come in, maybe through the back door, and killed your dad?"

Charlie sat there and looked Sam in the eye for a long moment. "Sometimes, like at night, I leave my door open just a little bit. Sometimes when I did that, I could hear the back door open and close. We always kept it locked, so whoever it was must've had a key. I asked my dad about it once, and he told me I better keep my door shut from then on."

Sam pursed his lips. "Do you think it might've been his girlfriend?"

Charlie shrugged. "I don't know," he said. "I guess it might have been."

"Charlie," Sam said, thinking about how he wanted to approach the subject, "I really can't leave you here like this. I'm going to need to take you with me to see a police detective, the one who talked to you that morning. She's a real good friend of mine, and she'll arrange for a place where you can stay, without getting into trouble. Will you come with me without making a fuss?"

Charlie looked at him, but didn't make any effort to get up and run away. “You're really a friend of my mom's?”

“Yes, I really am,” Sam said. “In fact, if you want, tomorrow I could arrange for you to see her. Would you like that?”

Charlie smiled. “Yeah, I would. Do we need to go see the detective tonight? Like, now?”

Sam nodded. “Yeah, I think we better. If you stay here, it could get Cindy and her parents in trouble, and we don't want that, now, do we?”

Charlie shook his head again. “No, I don't want to get anybody in trouble. Let me get my stuff, and I'm ready to go.” Charlie got up quickly, handed Sam the bag that still had part of the second meal in it, and hurried into the garage again. By the time Sam got to his feet, the boy was back. He had an overstuffed backpack on his shoulders, and Sam helped him get into the Ridgeline and buckle up.

As soon as Sam got behind the wheel, he took out his phone and called Karen.

“Sam? Is that you?” Karen asked.

“Yeah, Karen, it's me. I've got Charlie McAlester with me, and we need to come and talk to you. You're probably gonna want to contact CPS, because he really doesn't want to go back to his grandparents.”

“Holy crap, Sam, how do you do this stuff? I've got every cop in thirty miles looking for that kid, and we haven't turned up even a lead."

Sam smirked. "I got a message from a ghost, and that's all I'm gonna tell you. A guy has to have some secrets, right?"

Karen hesitated for a second. "Sam, you do know that there are people in the department who think you're just a little bit crazy, right? I've got to confess that I'm starting to be one of them. Okay, fine, come on over to my house. You know where it is?"

"Yeah, I remember. We'll be there in about fifteen minutes."

11

Karen opened the door as soon as Sam pulled into the driveway, and waited for him to walk Charlie up onto the porch. "Well, hello, Charlie," she said. "I've had a lot of people out looking for you. I'm glad to see you're safe."

Charlie looked down at his feet. "I'm sorry," he said. "I didn't mean to make trouble."

Karen stood aside and let them enter the house. "I'm not worried about that," she said. "We were just all worried that something bad might have happened to you."

Charlie shrugged and shook his head. "I just had to get away from my grandma and grandpa. All they talk about is how they want my mom to go to the electric chair, and every time I said I wanted to talk to her they got mad at me. My mom isn't a bad person."

Sam and Charlie sat on the couch, but Karen took a

seat across from them. Her daughter, a girl of about fifteen, came into the room with cans of soft drinks and offered them around. Sam and Charlie gratefully accepted.

"Charlie, when we talked the other day, there at your house, you told me that your mom killed your dad. Has something happened to change your mind about that?"

Charlie shrugged. "I'm not really sure what happened," he said. "The only thing I know for sure is that she wouldn't have done it unless she had a good reason. But me and Mr. Prichard have been talking, and now I'm not so sure she did. I was in my room and it's real hard to hear what's going on in the house from there."

"Yes, I heard about that," Karen said. "Mr. Prichard and one of our officers actually tried it, and found out that he couldn't hear what was going on in the living room very well at all, with your door closed. Do you have any other idea what might have happened to your dad?"

Charlie shook his head again. "I don't know. Mr. Prichard asked me if maybe somebody else might have come in, while my mom was gone. Like I said, I couldn't hear very well from inside my room, but I know that sometimes people come in the back door."

Karen glanced at Sam, then looked back to Charlie. "What kind of people?" she asked.

"Well, sometimes his girlfriend came in that way, but

I think there were other people who had a key, too. We always kept the back door locked, so whoever came in that way had to have a key."

"Do you think anyone came in the back door that morning?"

"I don't know about that," Charlie said. "The only times I ever heard the back door open was when I had my bedroom door open a little bit. I never saw who came in, though."

Karen looked at him for a moment. "Why do you think there were other people besides your dad's girlfriend who came in that way?"

Charlie hesitated for a moment. "Well, sometimes I'd hear the door open and close because I had my door open a little bit, and then I would hear somebody talking. Sometimes it wasn't a girl talking, sometimes it was a man."

Karen nodded. "And could you hear what they were saying?"

Charlie shook his head. "Uh-uh," he said. "Sometimes I'd hear somebody say my dad's name, but that was about all I could make out."

"And what about his girlfriend? Who is she?"

"I don't know, my dad always made me go in my room whenever she was supposed to come over. He said I was too young to know her."

Karen glanced at Sam, who shrugged. "You never heard your dad use her name or anything?"

"No, he just called her his Sweetie Pie. I only saw her once, from the back, and it was dark in the room. I think her hair was black or brown, and it was pretty long. That's all I know."

Karen thought for a moment, and then changed her tack. "Charlie, tell me more about why you didn't want to stay with your grandparents."

Charlie shrugged again. "They were just mean, every time they talked about my mom. It's like they hate her. I mean, I know they think she killed my dad, but they don't think about the things that he did."

Sam and Karen both raised their eyebrows. "What kind of things, Charlie?" Sam asked.

Charlie pulled his head down, as if trying to hide from the question. He sat there in silence for more than a minute, but neither Sam nor Karen said anything more. The silence bore down on the boy, and finally he looked up at Sam.

"My dad hurt people," Charlie said. "I heard him talking about it a couple of times, about how he had to go and make people do stuff. He said it was funny, how people would cry and beg when he was breaking their arms or something."

"Was he telling you about it?" Karen asked. "Or was he talking to someone else?"

Charlie hesitated again but only for a couple of seconds. "He was on the phone. I don't know who he was talking to. I told my grandma and grandpa, but they said I was making it up."

Karen looked at the boy for a moment, then glanced at Sam. "Sam, Charlie looks like he's pretty tired, don't you think?"

Sam nodded and grinned. "Yeah, I think sleeping on the concrete floor last night probably wasn't too comfortable, was it, Charlie?"

Charlie shook his head. "No, sir," he said. "But I don't think I would have gotten any sleep, anyway. I was trying to figure out how to go save my mom."

"Charlie," Karen said, "my son Michael has bunk beds. Would you like to get some sleep, and we can talk more about this tomorrow morning?"

Charlie nodded without speaking, and Karen called her son down from his room. The boy was a little younger than his sister, and Sam was surprised to see how much he looked like his late father.

"Michael, this is Charlie. He's going to stay with us tonight, so why don't you take him upstairs so he can get a shower, and then show him your room so he can get to bed."

Michael nodded and smiled at Charlie. "Sure, mom. Hey, Charlie, come on with me."

Charlie picked up his backpack and followed Michael up the stairs. Karen waited until they had gotten out of earshot before she turned to Sam.

"I called the Department of Human Services right after you called me, and told them I was probably going to keep Charlie here tonight." She gave Sam an exasperated sigh. "What do you think you're doing to my investigation? Sam, doggone it, you're throwing so many monkey wrenches into my works that I may have to start all over."

Sam shrugged. "Would you rather see an innocent woman go to prison? I don't think Candy did this, Karen. From the things I've learned, especially this stuff we're hearing from Charlie tonight, I've got a feeling there was more than one person who might have wanted Carlos dead."

"Yeah, and probably starting with his girlfriend! What kind of man keeps his girlfriend secret from his kid?"

Sam started to shrug, but then he suddenly looked Karen in the eye. "What kind of man keeps his girlfriend secret from his son? I'll tell you what kind. It's the kind of man whose girlfriend is married to somebody else!"

Karen pursed her lips and nodded. "You may have just hit on it. So now we've got several other potential killers in the mix, including the girlfriend, probably her husband or boyfriend, goodness knows how many people Carlos has bullied, and then there's the mystery man who comes to visit and maybe also talks to Carlos on the phone. And that doesn't even touch on what's going to happen when I tell the prosecutor that my one and only witness is no longer sure of his statement."

"They're not going to cut her loose, not yet," Sam said. "I don't know who you got on the prosecutor's table..."

"It's Monica Purvis," Karen said. "She's a bear, she's got political ambitions."

"Okay, well, she's undoubtedly going to claim that Charlie is changing his story, and go with the first interview you did with him on camera. That video will carry a lot of weight with the jury, so she's going to figure she can discredit Charlie's recant."

"True. Which means that you and I have a lot of work to do."

"I'm already working on it," Sam said. "With what Charlie has given us tonight, I'm going to start beating the bushes to find the girlfriend, and go back and talk to Carlos's coworkers. Hopefully I can get somebody to give me a lead on whoever he was breaking legs for."

"Good. I'll be doing some similar things. Oh, incidentally, you wanted to know about the cases where witnesses suddenly changed their minds, right? I put together a list for you, but I forgot it at the office. If you come by in the morning, I'll give it to you."

"I'll be there. By the way, I told Charlie that I could arrange for him to see his mom tomorrow. Can you set that up?"

Karen nodded. "Yeah, no problem. It might even do me a little good to watch how they interact. Maybe Charlie will say something to her that he wouldn't say to us."

Sam thanked her, and got up to leave. His hip was giving him trouble again, and he had to lean heavily on the cane as he walked out to the Ridgeline. He put the truck in gear and backed out of the driveway, then called Indie as he headed for home.

The call went to voicemail, so he just left a message saying that he loved her and Kenzie. He got to the house a few minutes later and went inside to sleep on his couch again.

At eight thirty the next morning, Sam pulled into the parking lot at Davidson lumber. The same clerk directed him back to the docks to find Dean and Leon, and Sam got the impression that he wasn't a bit happy to see the private detective coming back. Sam ignored him and went through the doors to the yard.

Dean was on the forklift, this time, while Leon was holding a clipboard and checking off items that were being loaded onto a truck. Sam walked up to him and held out his ID.

"Leon Schmidt? I'm Sam Prichard, private investigator."

Leon nodded once. "Yeah, I'd heard you were around asking questions the other day. Don't think I've got anything to say."

Sam put steel into his eyes. "Do you really think you want to take an attitude like that with me? I'm trying to find out who really killed Carlos McAlester, because I'm pretty darn sure his ex-wife didn't do it. Trouble is, she's the one sitting in jail and facing the possibility of death row. Now, she seems to think of you as a friend of hers, so I'm really hoping you're going to act like a friend and tell me whatever you can that might help her."

Leon kept looking at his clipboard, speaking out of the corner of his mouth. "Look, man, Carlos was not a nice guy, but he was an absolute choirboy compared to the people he worked for. As far as I know, Carlos never killed anybody, but I'm pretty sure he would have, if they had told him to. I'm also pretty sure that it wouldn't be the first time those people wanted somebody permanently out of the way, know what I mean? I've got a wife and kids, man, I can't afford to have them people mad at me."

"Look, I can understand exactly what you're saying." He took out the crosshaired photo of Kenzie and showed it briefly to Leon. "That's my little girl, and I had to take drastic measures to make sure these people couldn't get to her, so I'm with you. I'm not asking you to point fingers or testify, I'm just looking for a lead. Can you give me anything I can use to try to figure out who those people are?"

Leon checked off a couple more items, then turned slightly toward Sam, his voice down to a whisper. "Gerald Pennington," he said softly. "He can tell you more than I could, and he's not nearly as afraid to talk as I am. That's all I got, and I'd appreciate it if you don't come back."

"Cool," Sam whispered back. "Now, cuss me out and throw me out of this place. Loudly."

Leon looked at the clipboard for another second, then turned around and looked Sam in the eye. "I told you, I got nothing to say to you," he yelled. "Now you either get lost, or I'm going to toss you right out on your ass! And don't come back!"

Sam pretended to be surprised at his outburst, called him a jerk and then turned around and stomped as well as he could back to the door into the store. He didn't even look at the clerk as he passed the counter, then pushed through the outer doors and headed for the Corvette. He pulled out of the driveway before he took out his phone.

He googled Gerald Pennington and found out that the name belonged to a remodeling contractor. He called the number listed and asked for an appointment to speak with the man, but Pennington invited him to come right on out to his current job site. Sam got the address and punched it into his GPS, and arrived only a half hour later.

12

Pennington saw the Corvette pull in and walked toward it as Sam got out. He extended a hand, and Sam shook it, then produced his ID.

"Mr. Pennington, I'm Sam Prichard, a private detective. I'm trying to get some information that may help me prove my client is innocent of a murder charge, and somebody told me you might be able to help."

Pennington looked him over for a moment, then smiled. "You working on the McAlester murder? Carlos? Normally I wouldn't say this, but it couldn't have happened to a more deserving guy. You ask me, whoever did it should have made him suffer more before he checked out."

Sam grinned. "I'm hearing that a lot lately," he said. "I take it you knew him?"

Pennington rolled up his left sleeve and Sam saw a thick surgical scar. "That's a reminder," he said. "Carlos paid me a visit about a year and a half ago, and when I told him to get lost he took my arm and broke it like a piece of kindling over the tailgate of my own truck. That probably wouldn't have done him much good, but then he threatened a couple of my employees with even worse things, so I finally agreed to go along with what he wanted."

Sam's eyebrows went up. "And what was it he wanted?"

Pennington looked around to make sure no one was in earshot, then turned back to Sam. "He wanted me to drop a lawsuit. See, my wife was killed by a drunk driver two-and-a-half years ago, and I had filed a wrongful death suit against the guy who did it. The driver was a local doctor, and somehow or other they managed to lose the breathalyzer report from the evening it happened. The doctor got slapped with a fine and his insurance company paid off fifty grand to me, but I wanted the SOB to pay. Since I couldn't do anything about getting any criminal charges brought back up on him, I filed a wrongful death suit for ten million. I didn't want the money, you understand, I just wanted the man who killed my wife to at least feel some impact over it." He glanced up at the sun, then took out a handkerchief and wiped the sweat off of his face. "Anyway, Carlos came around a couple of times telling me I should drop the lawsuit, that I should be content with what the insurance paid and let it go. I told him he could kiss my ass, that I wasn't backing down for any reason, and then he came back a third time. I was alone on a job site, and that's when he busted my arm. I told him I didn't give a crap how many bones he broke, there was no way I was going to drop that lawsuit, but then he showed me a picture. It was one of my drywall guys, with his family. Carlos asked me how I would feel if he and his kids were in a bad wreck of their own, and after what he had just done to my arm, I was pretty sure he'd follow through on that threat. I decided I didn't want anyone else to suffer because of me, so I took out my phone and called my lawyer, told him to drop the lawsuit. Then I went to the hospital and ended up in surgery, getting a couple of steel plates and a dozen screws put into my arm. Now I set off metal detectors everywhere I go."

Sam shook his head. "Mr. Pennington, do you have any idea how Carlos got involved in this? Did that doctor hire him?"

Pennington laughed, shaking his own head. "He didn't have to," he said. "All he had to do was call up Randy Whitaker. Whitaker's the one who sent Carlos to visit me."

Sam's eyes went wide, as the name registered. "Randy Whitaker? The county attorney?"

Pennington was nodding. "The very same," he said. "Whitaker came after me five years ago, before he was got the county job. I was building a strip mall down on Zuni Street, and he wanted me to go along with a modification to the property survey. He had a client who owned the property right next door, but he needed seven more feet of street frontage to qualify for some government grant or other. They offered me what was probably a fair price for the East End of my property, but that would have forced me to have a whole new building designed, parking lot and all. I turned them down, but Whitaker kept pushing the issue. The last time we talked about it, I told him he could forget it, but he said I ought to take the deal while I could. I asked him what he meant, and he said something about having Carlos explain it to me. Bet you can guess who showed up the next day, right?"

"Carlos McAlester," Sam said, and Pennington grinned and pointed a finger at him.

"Give that man a cigar," he said. "Carlos made it clear to me that if I didn't go along with the sale, I'd be looking at having some extremely bad luck in the near future. When I asked what kind of bad luck he was talking about, he just said it would be something that I didn't have enough insurance to cover. I wasn't quite as cocky back then as I am now, and I caved in. I sold that stupid little strip of land for thirty-eight thousand dollars, and then it cost me seventy thousand for a whole new architectural layout."

Sam settled himself onto the fender of the Corvette. "So maybe Whitaker hired whoever Carlos was working for. What makes you so sure that was Whitaker himself?"

"Because I know a half-dozen other people who went through the same thing when they butted heads with Whitaker. Sometimes it was just Carlos who came to see them, but a couple times Whitaker was with him. Randy Whitaker isn't just a lawyer, he's the worst kind of power broker that any city could ever have. If you want something to go your way, all you have to do is let Whitaker know about it, and not long after that you'll be quoted a price. If you're willing to pay, then whatever you wanted is what happens. I know for a fact that it's Whitaker who gets the money, and Whitaker who pays it out to the lowlife bastards like Carlos McAlester that he sends out to do the job."

"Is there a way to prove it, though?" Sam asked.

"What is it they say on the crime shows on TV? Follow the money. If you took a good look at Whitaker's bank account a few days before my arm got broken, I'll bet you'd see a pretty big deposit. You'd find another one in Carlos's account, probably the very next day."

"Mr. Pennington, I've spoken to a couple of people who tell me that Carlos wasn't the only one working for whoever was giving him orders. Any chance you know who else might have been in that racket?"

Pennington shrugged his shoulders. "I didn't have any direct experience with him, but I've heard other people talking about Roland Maxwell. Roland was special forces in the Army, and he's about as mean and vicious as a man can be. Never holds down any kind of regular job, but he's always got money, and I hear tell that a few people got him instead of Carlos. Even heard of one case when the two of them showed up together."

"Okay," Sam said, "can you give me the date when your arm got broken? I've got someone who can check those bank accounts."

"That's easy, it was January 19th of last year. I can remember so easily because it was a year to the day after the accident that killed my wife."

Sam scribbled the date in a notepad. "Can you think of anyone else who might talk to me about this? About dealings with Whitaker or McAlester?"

Pennington shook his head. "Not as long as Whitaker is still running around loose. I can tell you this, though. If you can get the prosecutor to go after him, I'm willing to testify. I'd just want some kind of protection for the people who work for me. I already know that Whitaker doesn't care who gets hurt, as long as he gets what he wants. He can send people after me all he wants, I got my concealed carry permit and I'm ready to put up a fight. I just don't want anyone else getting hurt because of me."

Sam thanked the man for his information and then got back into his car. It was still fairly early, but he had promised to go by Karen's office and pick up the list of witnesses she had prepared for him. He called ahead to make sure she was in, and she told him she'd be waiting.

"Come on in," Karen said when Sam tapped on her

door. He hobbled inside and sat heavily in the chair in front of her desk, and she passed him a manila envelope. He glanced inside and saw a list of names and contact information for each.

"Came by for this," he said, "but I've also got a little information for you. Talked with a fellow this morning who had a run-in with Carlos McAlester. McAlester wanted him to drop a lawsuit he had going against a local doctor who was driving drunk one night and killed this guy's wife. The case somehow never made it to the prosecutor, so he had filed a wrongful death suit. When he declined to drop it, McAlester broke his arm, seriously enough that it required surgery to put it back together."

Karen leaned back in her chair and looked at him. "The doctor hired McAlester?"

Sam shook his head. "According to my witness, McAlester worked for a man you probably know pretty well, Randy Whitaker. It seems that Whitaker considers himself something of a power broker. If you need something done, or not done as the case may be, you make a deal with Whitaker. He sends someone like Carlos to convince the people involved to do things his way. My guy had dealt with both Whitaker and Carlos before the arm-breaking incident, so he's pretty sure of his facts."

Karen's eyes had gone wide at the mention of Whitaker's name. "Sam, I'm going to be honest," she said. "There have been rumors for the last several years about Whitaker, but no one has ever gotten any kind of dirt on him. Personally, I think the guy is a sleazeball. When Ralph was killed, Whitaker was the lawyer the city hired to negotiate the settlement. He actually made a pass at me while we were in a meeting to discuss my kids' survivor benefits."

Sam grinned from ear to ear. "Well, the guy I talked to, who wants his name left out for the moment, gave me a lead that might tie Whitaker to Carlos McAlester. If I can find a few more connections, maybe from your list of witnesses, we could have enough to go to the prosecutor. Wouldn't break my heart a bit to put this bastard away. If I'm hearing it right, then he's the son of a bitch who sent me this."

He reached into his pocket and tossed the crosshair photo of Kenzie onto Karen's desk. She picked it up and looked at it, and Sam saw a flash of anger in her eyes before she got herself back under control.

"I wish you'd brought this to me when you got it? There might have been fingerprints on it, or DNA that we could trace."

Sam rolled his eyes. "I can't imagine anyone would be stupid enough to handle that photo without rubber gloves and a sterile environment. It came in a letter to Indie, with a computer-printed label."

"Still," Karen said, "you should've told me about it sooner, Sam."

"I told you about it yesterday. And just for the record, McAlester used a photo in a similar way to intimidate my source, once. You can bet your sweet ass I want to nail the guy who took that picture."

Karen looked at the picture again for a moment, then handed it back to Sam. "Whatever you get on Whitaker, I want to hear about it. If you're right, then he's an accessory after the fact to multiple crimes, including several homicides. On the other hand, if I go upstairs with this right now, he's going to hear about it. I think it would be best if I let you handle this for right now, don't you?"

"I think you're right," Sam said. "I'm going to call Indie and have her get on some computerized aspects, and as soon as I have something concrete, you'll know it."

"I expect to hear from you no matter what you find, even if it's muddy and runny. Like I told you, there's been a lot of rumors about Whitaker, but no one has ever been able to make anything stick. If anybody can, I think it's you, but that doesn't mean you won't need some help. And don't forget—we're talking about a man who uses threats and intimidation as part of his daily business. If he's as bad as we think he is and finds out you're coming his way, he won't hesitate to have you eliminated."

Sam shrugged. "If there's one thing I've learned in the last couple of years, it's that I'm an extremely hard son of a bitch to kill. I don't plan on letting that change anytime soon."

Sam got up and left the office, leaning on his cane as he made his way out to the car. As soon as he was sitting behind the wheel, he took out his phone and called his wife.

A sleepy voice answered. "Hey, baby..."

Sam grinned, but kept it out of his voice. "Hi, sweetheart," he said. "I'm so sorry to be calling this early, I know you've got to be exhausted, but when you're up and about I need you to get Herman on to some things for me. Are you awake enough for me to tell you what it is, or should I text it to you?"

"Sam Prichard, we've been married over a year. Am I ever ready to function right after I wake up? Text me whatever you need, and I'll put Herman on it once I'm awake." She paused for a second, then went on. "Unless you need it right now? I could probably force myself to get up, if you need me to."

Sam couldn't help it, he laughed. "Baby, go ahead and get some rest. The information I need will be just as valuable this afternoon as it would be right now. Besides, I'm still working so I may have more leads to give you by the time you get up and drink some coffee."

"Okay," Indie sighed. "I'll call you when I'm up and about, okay?"

Sam told her that would be fine, and let her get off the phone. He texted her Randy Whitaker's name and asked her to check his bank accounts for a large deposit somewhere around the date Pennington had given him, and then cross-reference it with deposits to Carlos's account. He sent the message and tucked the phone back into his pocket, then pulled the list Karen had given him out of the envelope. He scanned down the names, and suddenly one of them jumped out at him.

Jim Mitchell. Sam checked the address to be sure it was the one he knew, and then fired up the car.

13

The Corvette cruised past Sam's own house and pulled in at the Mitchells' place a couple of blocks down. Jim and Anita Mitchell were friends, and Sam had known them since shortly after his retirement from the police force. Sam was in a wheelchair at the time, and his grass had been growing pretty long. Early one morning he heard the sound of a lawnmower outside and looked out to see Jim and another neighbor cutting the grass for him. He'd gone outside to thank them and offer to pay, but they told him that was what neighbors were for, and he and Jim became good friends. Jim and Anita had often invited him to join them and their kids for dinner, or to go out to a movie. When Indie had come into his life, she and Anita had also hit it off, while Kenzie found the Mitchell twins, who were close to her age, to be the perfect playmates.

According to the papers in the envelope, Jim had

been a witness in a murder case a year before Sam had met him. The case involved the death of a teenage girl who was last seen trying to get away from an older man in a Lincoln Navigator. Jim was one of two witnesses who had seen the girl through the truck's window, slapping at the glass and screaming for help. Jim had gotten a partial license number and called police, and the truck was traced to a local businessman named Harold Morgan.

The girl's body was found the next morning, dumped behind a trash bin at a fast food restaurant. She was identified as the daughter of a minister from Utah, and had been missing for over a week from her home. Jim was called to the morgue to confirm that she was the girl he had seen crying for help.

The Navigator and its owner were located later that day, and it was confirmed that he had recently returned from Salt Lake City, but the man swore ignorance about anything to do with the girl. Unfortunately, neither Jim nor the other witness had gotten a truly good look at the man who was driving the Navigator, but when Jim saw Morgan in profile, he was confident enough to say that he could make a positive identification. Along with the statements of both witnesses that Morgan's Navigator was the one they had seen the girl in, and with the partial plate that Jim had gotten, the case looked pretty solid. All that remained was to put Morgan on trial.

Four days before the trial was set to begin, however, both of the witnesses suddenly declared that they were unsure of their identification. They apologized for wasting the time of the police, but there was nothing the prosecutor's office could do. Without their testimony, it was impossible to prove that Morgan had had anything to do with the girl's death or disappearance.

Sam parked his Corvette next to Jim's Mustang and got out. He made his way up the walk to the door and rang the bell, but Anita snatched it open even before he got his finger off the button.

"Hi, Sam," she said. "You looking for Jim?"

"Yeah," Sam answered. "I called his office, but his secretary said he was off today. Is he around?"

"Sure, come on in. He's out in the backyard, we got family coming in this evening and he's getting the grill ready for a cookout."

Sam thanked her and went through the house to the back sliding door. Jim was on the deck, just outside, and he looked up with a smile when he saw Sam.

"Hey, buddy, how's it going?"

Sam took the hand that Jim extended and shook it firmly. "Kind of hectic, right now, to be honest," Sam said. "You probably haven't heard, but my bass player is in jail on a murder charge, so I've sort of come out of retirement. I'm pretty certain she didn't do it, but the prosecutor thinks she murdered her ex-husband, and this case has taken a turn that got me digging into some other things."

"Oh, gee, Sam, I'm sorry to hear that. Knowing you,

though, I would just about bet you're feeling like you're back in your element, am I right?"

Sam grinned. "Maybe you know me too well," he said. "Listen, Jim, this case is the reason I stopped by. I was looking into some things that might be connected to it and your name came up."

Jim looked up from where he was cleaning the gas jets on the grill, and Sam saw wariness come into his eyes. "My name? In a murder case?"

"Well, not precisely in connection with this case, no. The thing is, the man who was killed in this case is someone you might have known, or met at one time. His name was Carlos McAlester. Ring any bells?"

Jim's eyes suddenly found the grill fascinating. "That, um, that doesn't sound familiar. Why do you think I might have known him?"

Sam glanced over to his right and saw a deck chair, which he pulled close and sank into. "Carlos McAlester was what we call a leg breaker. He used violence, or the threat of violence, to intimidate people into doing what he wanted them to do. Things like backing down on a lawsuit, or suddenly forgetting details about a case he was supposed to testify in. Jim, you were supposed to testify in a murder case a while back. In the initial stages, you made it clear that you were absolutely certain of your identification of the suspect, but just before his trial was set to begin you decided you weren't so sure after all. It seems like that's been happening a lot lately, and now that we know about McAlester and his escapades, it's a safe bet that he had something to do with a lot of those situations."

Sam paused and just looked at his friend, who continued fiddling with the grill. "Sam," Jim began, "I, um, I don't think I ever met the guy. As for what happened in that other case, I just—I just couldn't be sure that I had the right guy. That's all it was."

Sam sat in silence as Jim continued what he was doing. After a moment, Jim started talking again. "Anyway, you know me. I wouldn't let somebody scare me off."

Sam reached into his pocket and took out the photo of Kenzie, holding it out so Jim could see it. His friend looked at the picture, then turned his eyes away again quickly.

"Jim, I know what kind of man McAlester was, and I know that he isn't the only one. These men, they don't just threaten to get rough with you to get what they want, they'll threaten your family, your children...Jim, talk to me. Tell me what really happened."

Jim set the grates back on the grill and then walked over and took another chair. He looked down at the deck for a few seconds, then leaned back to let his eyes meet Sam's.

"Yeah, it was McAlester, but he had some other guy with him. Roland something or other. They caught me while I was out to lunch one day and showed me several pictures like that, pictures of Anita and the twins. They told me in no uncertain terms that there was nothing I could do to protect my family, and if I didn't change my story then something terrible would happen to them." He closed his eyes and put a hand over his mouth. When he spoke again, his voice was muffled. "Sam, I'm not a coward, I swear I'm not, but you and I both know that a man won't risk his family if he can avoid it. I knew it wasn't right to change my story, and I really wanted that monster to get what was coming to him, but I just couldn't take a chance that something would happen to Anita or the kids."

"Hey," Sam said, "don't worry, Jim, you're preaching to the choir. As soon as I saw this photograph, I called in some pretty huge favors to get Indie and Kenzie completely out of the state and with extremely efficient bodyguards. I don't mind facing down people like this, myself, but like you say, I'm not going to put my family at risk in order to do it. I'm not going to look down on you, Jim. I just need to know the details."

Jim swallowed hard and let his hand drop to his lap. "Like I told you, they came at me on my lunch break. Carlos, he did all the talking, he told me that somebody powerful wanted me to decide not to testify. I told him to get lost at first, I really did, but then that other guy, Roland, he pulled the pictures out of his pocket and just handed them to me. He didn't say a word, but Carlos leaned real close to me and whispered something about bad things happening to my family if I didn't change my mind."

"Did either of them give you any idea who this powerful person might be?"

"No names were mentioned, but it was pretty obvious. It had to have been that guy Morgan, he's the one who was looking at life in prison."

Sam chewed the inside of his cheek for a second. "Well, it turns out there's somebody who's running these thugs. A guy like Morgan, he wants witnesses to decide they don't want to talk, he tells this other guy and that fellow sends out the leg breakers. I've already got an idea who that person is, I'm just trying to find proof."

Jim shook his head. "I wouldn't know anything about that, all I know is that I wasn't going to let them hurt my family. I hated backing down, Sam, but I just didn't feel like I had a choice."

Sam nodded. "I understand. Does Anita know?"

Jim let his eyes drop to the floor again. "Yeah, she knows. When I told her that I had to back out of testifying, she went through the roof. I finally had to tell her why, so she wouldn't think I was just a piece of crap."

Sam grinned at his friend. "You're not a piece of crap, Jim. You stepped up when you saw that girl in trouble, and you tried to help. Then you were willing to testify against the man who probably killed her. That's not the way a coward does things, and you don't have to be a coward to choose the safety of your family over civic duty." He got to his feet, leaning on the table to do so.

"I'm gonna go," he said. "Right now, I'm thinking that powerful somebody is probably behind the murder of Carlos McAlester, and that's why I'm trying to build a case against him. If I can find enough connections, then maybe I can shake somebody up enough to talk." He held out a hand to shake again, and Jim took it.

"You're not going to tell Anita we talked about this, are you?" Jim asked.

"Nothing to tell," Sam said. "I just stopped by because I was bored."

Sam walked down the steps from the deck and around the house, opening the gate to get out of the fenced backyard. He got back into his car and looked at the list again. The next recanted witness he wanted to visit was a woman named Mabel Swinson, and she lived only a few blocks away.

Mabel Swinson was a feisty old lady of almost 70, and she had contacted police about drug trafficking that was going on right in front of her own house. Using an iPhone, she had actually gotten video of drug transactions taking place, and when the dealers were rounded up she had agreed to testify against them.

Like Jim, she had suddenly had a change of heart just a few days before she was due to testify. Her excuse was that her memory wasn't as good as it had been when she was young, and she couldn't remember for sure just whom she had seen selling drugs. When she was shown the video she herself had taken, she insisted that she couldn't remember doing so.

The video would have still been fairly damning evidence on its own, but without eyewitness testimony as to when and where it had been created, it wouldn't have been terribly difficult for a defense attorney to get it thrown out. The prosecutor had finally decided to dismiss the charges, and Mrs. Swinson's home was vandalized several times over the next few weeks.

Sam found her out in her garden, down on her knees and carefully pulling the weeds that were threatening to choke out her late-summer crops. He introduced himself and showed her his ID, and she smiled as she invited him to come and sit on the porch.

Once they were seated, Sam asked her why she had changed her mind about testifying, and at first she gave him the same song and dance about getting old and losing her memory that she had given to the prosecutor. When Sam mentioned Carlos McAlester, though, the look in her eyes told him he had struck pay dirt.

"That boy," she said, "he a bad'n. Why, I want you to know he come up in here, right up in my house, and he told me if I didn't shut my mouth, he was gonna shut it for me for good. I told him, I said I'm an old woman, I done lived a long time and I ain't afraid of him or nobody else. He said he didn't figure I'd be afraid of him for myself, but then he reminded me I got kids and grandkids and great-grandkids, and he made it clear if I didn't forget about what I seen, he was gon' go after them." Suddenly she had a tear running down each cheek. "That's why I changed my story. I didn't forget nothin', but I had to take care of my family, you know?"

Sam nodded, and showed her the photo. "I do know, I know exactly what you mean. Somebody is trying to make me stop asking questions, but I was able to make sure my family was safe, so I'm still asking. Mrs. Swinson, do you have any idea who might have sent him to see you?"

"I know exactly who it was," she said. "I told my daughter Melanie about it, she works down at the City Hall, and she said it was the lawyer them boys hired."

Sam's eyes lit up. "And did you happen to get his name?"

The old woman nodded her head. "I sure did," she said. "It was the one as got the big county job, now, name of Whitaker."

Sam thanked her and made his way back to the car. He had just backed out of her driveway when his phone rang. It was Indie calling, and he answered quickly.

"Sam," Indie said without preamble, "you were right. Whitaker got a big deposit, almost thirty thousand, on the seventeenth of that month. On the twentieth, Carlos McAlester deposited ninety-five hundred dollars to his account."

"That's fantastic, Babe," Sam said. "You got a pencil and paper handy? I got several more for you to look over."

He read off the dates relevant to the list of recanted witnesses, and Indie fed the information into Herman. Since Herman had already hacked its way into Whitaker's and McAlester's bank accounts, it only took him a few minutes to correlate the data.

"Okay, you gave me eighteen dates. On fourteen of them, Whitaker made a deposit to his account within two or three days before, and McAlester made one the day after. I'm starting to see a pattern, here, Sam."

"I see it, too," Sam said. "Okay, here's another name. Roland Maxwell, lives over on Shoshone. See if you can find a bank account for him, and whether any of those dates precede a deposit to his accounts."

"Okay, but that will take a little more time. Do you know how many banks there are in Denver? Way too many. I'll set Herman to digging, but then we're fixing to head out to the Universal Studios Park. Or do you need this like ASAP?"

"No, that's okay. It'll just be more evidence of Whitaker's involvement in McAlester's activities, and if we can take down another of his leg breakers, so much the better. You girls go on and have some fun. How's your security detail holding up?"

Indie laughed. "Jennifer is doing fine, but the men are all taking turns being wrapped around Kenzie's little finger. You haven't seen anything until you've seen three heavily armed men riding on the spinning teacups. Two of them are constantly watching around for any trouble, while the third one is doing everything he can think of to spoil your daughter rotten. I had to threaten one of them yesterday, he was trying to buy her a third bag of cotton candy."

"Yeah, well, tell them not to spoil her too much, that's my job."

Sam talked to Kenzie for a moment, and heard an entirely different version of the spinning teacup story in which she made it spin so fast that all three of the men turned green. He told her to spin it even faster next time, make sure they really felt it. After a moment, she gave the phone back to her mother, and Sam and Indie said their goodbyes.

The phone hadn't even made it back into his pocket before it rang again, however. This time it was Karen Parks calling.

"Hello," Sam said.

"Sam, I took Charlie in to visit his mother this morning," Karen said. "He told her that you helped him figure out that she probably wasn't the one who killed his dad. Sam, I was amazed at how much that kid loves his mother. Anyway, after I heard that, I had to go to the prosecutor and explain that our chief witness wasn't going to be reliable."

"Oh-oh," Sam said. "How did she take it?"

"Monica? How do you think, she went through the roof! She actually tried to tell me that Ms. McAlester had sent someone to scare the kid into changing his story. I made it quite clear that I knew better than that, and that in my opinion, we've got the wrong person in jail. She told me to keep my opinions to myself."

"Well, I didn't figure that would be enough to get Candy out," Sam said. "On the other hand, her attorney will have a field day with it. Your prosecutor should know there's no way she's going to get a conviction, not with all the issues with evidence and the other possibilities."

"I told you, Monica is a politician. She's not going to give up until we hand her proof of Ms. McAlester's innocence, or a locked-up case against the real killer. And speaking of that, are you getting anywhere?"

"I'm coming up with enough to show a pattern, that Whitaker would receive a large payment just before one of your witnesses changed his story, and McAlester or another leg breaker would have a chunk of money the day after. I can even tie Whitaker directly to a couple of cases. I'm just trying to find the missing link that connects him to Carlos's murder. Right now, I'm thinking that maybe Carlos became a liability in some way, and Whitaker had him taken out of the equation. You can help me out a little bit, if you can figure out where Roland Maxwell was on the day McAlester was killed."

"Roland Maxwell? I know that name, where do I know that name from? I can't think of it right now, but it'll come to me. Let me get off the stupid phone, and I'll see what I can find out."

"Hey, so what's going to happen to Charlie?"

"Well, since he insists on not going back to his grandparents, DHS says he has to go into a foster care situation for now. They took him after the visit, and he'll be staying in one of the group homes for a while."

"I'll bet that's gonna suck," Sam said. "You never hear anything good about the foster care system. Okay, I'll let you go for now. Hopefully one of us will come up with something soon."

Sam tucked the phone into his pocket again, and drove the Corvette to the next address on his list.

14

The next three people Sam talked to wouldn't tell him anything, and he began to get frustrated. The only hope he felt he had for proving Candy innocent was to find out who actually killed her ex-husband, and he was pretty convinced that it had to have been Whitaker or one of his people. Without more to go on, however, there was not much chance he'd be able to prove it.

After leaving the last of the three, Sam was feeling discouraged. It was already past noon, and he was getting hungry, so he pulled into a Taco Bell and ordered lunch. He picked it up at the window and decided to simply sit in the car and eat.

He had just finished eating when a car pulled into the parking slot to his right, and a well-dressed man got out and opened the passenger door of the Corvette. Before Sam could react, he had sat down in the car with him, and Sam saw the gun in his hand.

"Mr. Prichard," the man said, "allow me to introduce myself. My name is Randall Whitaker, and I understand you're asking some questions about me."

Sam looked at Whitaker. "This is a little out of character for you, isn't it? Actually coming after someone yourself, rather than sending one of your soldiers?"

Whitaker smiled. "I'm here myself, Mr. Prichard—may I call you Sam? I'm here myself, Sam, because you and I have some mutual interests. You're trying to find out who killed Carlos McAlester, and so am I. I thought it might be smart if we work together, rather than becoming enemies."

"Whitaker, I know enough about you and what you're doing to make the thought of doing anything with you cause me to be ill." He reached slowly into his pocket and withdrew the photo of Kenzie. "After getting this, what could possibly make you think I'd be willing to work with you in any way?"

Whitaker's eyebrows lowered, and he took the photo from Sam's hand. He looked at it carefully, and then raised his eyes back to Sam's face. "This is not my doing, Sam," he said. "Someone else is trying to scare you off, not me. I can assure you I don't want you to drop this case." He passed the picture back.

Sam watched his face carefully. "Why is that? Isn't it likely to expose you and the things you do?"

"Since you know what I do, you know that I tend to always get what I want, so that doesn't worry me. Now, here's the situation, Sam. I didn't kill Carlos, nor did I have him killed. Good grief, why on earth would I get rid of the tool that had made me more money than anything else? Carlos was excellent at what he did, and he had a particular knack for making evidence disappear, or making it say what we wanted it to say. It will be a long time before I find anyone who can fill his shoes. The problem for me is that, since I didn't have him killed, the very fact that he is dead causes me some worry. I think we both know his ex-wife didn't do it, simply because there was enough animosity between them that he would never have let her get close to him with a knife in her hand."

"He let somebody," Sam said. "Maybe he just didn't see it coming."

"I'm going to tell you something that not many people know," Whitaker said. "Carlos McAlester was probably one of the toughest men I've ever met in my life. I've seen him take down as many as a half-dozen opponents at once, and all without ever touching a weapon of any kind. It was sort of a pride thing with him, that he never used anything but his own hands and feet. I've seen people pull knives on him, even a gun once, and each time he simply took it away and then proceeded to beat the guy senseless. For anyone to get close enough to stick a knife into his chest, we absolutely have to be talking about someone he was foolish enough to trust completely. That wouldn't have been his ex-wife."

Sam sat there and looked at Whitaker for a moment, letting the things he was hearing tumble about inside his head. If Whitaker was telling the truth, then Carlos would've been a hard man to kill under any circumstances. The theory that the killer had to have been someone Carlos trusted was once again making a lot of sense.

"Any idea who he might've trusted that much?"

Whitaker shrugged. "I can think of a very few people, one of them being myself. A couple of others are men like him who work for me, but neither of them would have any reason to want Carlos dead. Quite the opposite, because any time they needed backup, it was always Carlos they asked for. There is no way they would have done anything like this. Even if they were jealous of him, it would have been biting off their nose to spite their face."

Sam chewed on his bottom lip for a moment. "The kid, Charlie, he mentioned that Carlos had a girlfriend, but he didn't know who it was. Do you?"

Whitaker's eyebrows went up. "A girlfriend? He had dozens of them; the guy could get just about any woman he wanted. He dated models, doctors, lawyers, even one girl who works for the cops, but as far as I know, none of them were anything serious. If he had a steady girl, I don't know anything about her."

"He seems to have had one, but he didn't let his son meet her, or even know her name. My guess is that she was probably married or involved with someone," Sam said, "because he kept Charlie out of sight whenever she came over. The kid always had to go to his room and close the door. He said he snuck out once and saw her from the back, but all he knew is that she had long dark hair."

Whitaker shook his head. "Like I said, I don't know anything about her. Carlos and I weren't exactly friends, and we didn't run in the same circles."

Sam nodded, and took a different angle. "Okay, you say you're trying to figure out who killed him, too. What about the girl at the coffee shop drive-through? When I asked her if she had seen Candy, and I can't believe anybody could forget that hair, it was pretty obvious to me the girl was afraid to admit that she'd been there. Someone warned her about talking. That wasn't you, either?"

"Nope," Whitaker said. "Look, I've got no interest in seeing an innocent woman go down for this murder. I want to know who actually did it, because if it was in any way related to—let's just say, related to my activities—then I need to know who I'm dealing with. Maybe you should put some pressure on that girl to find out who scared her off. Sounds to me like there might be a connection to the killer."

"Yeah, I thought of the same thing. I'll be visiting her shortly." He cocked his head to one side and looked Whitaker in the eye. "You do know that the cops are on to you, now, right? And not just because of me; they've been hearing rumors about you for a while. You send your muscle to intimidate witnesses, force people to sell what they don't want to sell. You can't get away with things forever."

Whitaker grinned. "Rumors don't worry me, and anyone you've been talking to won't be willing to testify. You can trust me on that, and take it to the bank. I'm pretty well insulated, Sam, and well enough entrenched that you'd never get a prosecutor to take me on, anyway. One of the nice things about being the go-to guy for the wealthy and influential is that you always know where plenty of bodies are buried. You might have stumbled across a few cases where my fingerprints might show up, but there are hundreds more you'll never find. Let's just say that some of those involve the very people who would make the final decisions about whether to mess with me."

Sam sat quietly for a moment, then grinned. "So you're untouchable, then, right? Okay, fine. If I can't bring you down, then I want you in my debt. I'll find out who killed Carlos, but you owe me a favor. Fair enough?"

Whitaker laughed out loud. "Oh, Sam, I knew you were a lot more like me than you let on. Deal! You find out who killed Carlos and make sure they can't bother me in the future, and I'll give you not just one favor, but two. Doesn't matter what they are, you need something done, I'll get it done."

Sam nodded and held out a hand. "Good enough. Just one caveat on this—if I ever find out that you've actually had someone killed to accomplish your goals, all bets are off. I'll come after you with everything I've got."

Whitaker shook Sam's hand. "That's the one thing I'll never do," he said. "Believe it or not, I don't think I could live with myself if I went that far. I like power, but not at the expense of a life." He turned and got out of the Corvette, slid back into the driver seat of his own car and backed out.

Sam continued to sit in his car for a moment, thinking over the conversation he had just had with Whitaker. If there was one thing Sam Prichard didn't believe, it was that any criminal could truly be untouchable. He may have to wait a while to nail Whitaker's hide to the wall, but he promised himself that the day would come when he would see the man standing before a judge who wasn't afraid of him.

On the other hand, if he was telling the truth, then Sam now knew that he could eliminate Whitaker and his cronies from his list of suspects. That didn't really narrow the field, since Whitaker himself seemed to think that the killer might have been someone connected to one of the people he had pressured.

Pressure. That reminded Sam of the girl at the coffee shop, and he started the Corvette and backed it out of the slot. Sammy's was only a short distance away, and Sam was walking up to the counter only fifteen minutes later.

There was a different girl at the counter. "Hi, and welcome to Sammy's."

Sam smiled. "Hi, there. Is Brittany around?"

The girl nodded. "Yeah, just a moment, she's in the back." She turned and stuck her head through a doorway. "Brittany! There's someone here looking for you."

"Just a sec," Sam heard Brittany call out. He stepped to his right so that a new customer who had come in behind him could get to the counter. Brittany came to the doorway with a smile, but she lost it the moment she saw Sam.

For a split second, Sam thought she was going to turn and run, but then she steeled herself and walked up to him. "You were looking for me?" Brittany asked him defiantly. "I already told you, I never saw that girl."

Sam smiled and nodded. "Yes, I know you did," he said softly. "The trouble is, I also know you're lying, and that makes me think someone has told you that lying is the thing you should do. Now, you seem like a pretty nice girl, and I'd hate to see you get in trouble for withholding evidence in a murder investigation. The way I understand it, that can get you a pretty serious prison sentence, like two or three years. I've got a feeling you can't afford that kind of trouble, so I thought I'd come back and give you a chance to get out of it."

Brittany's eyes went wide. "I—I-I'm not lying," she

whispered. "I don't know why you would think I am, because I'm not. I absolutely did not see that girl last Sunday morning."

Sam shook his head. "Look, Brittany, you can talk to me and we keep this quiet, or I can call Detective Parks at the homicide division of the Police Department, and you can talk to her. If you talk to her, she's likely to have you charged with obstructing justice, just because you didn't own up sooner. There's no way in the world you're going to get out of this, unless you tell me the truth, right now."

Brittany looked around the room, and noticed that the other barista was watching her out of the corner of her eye. She turned back to Sam and motioned with her head for him to follow her, then went to a table in the far back corner of the room. She sat down with her back to the wall, and Sam took the seat across from her.

"Look, I really didn't want to be involved in this mess, anyway," she said. "When the cops first called and asked me about that lady, I just didn't want to get involved, you know? That's why I said I didn't remember her coming in."

Sam watched her face as she spoke, and got the impression she might be telling him the truth. "So, nobody asked you to keep your mouth shut about this? If they did, you need to be honest with me about it, Brittany. That would mean that person is somehow involved in the murder, and covering up for them would make you an accessory. That alone is enough to get you sent to prison."

The girl closed her eyes for just a moment, then opened them, and Sam saw tears starting to well up. "Look, I just told you the truth. I really didn't want to get involved, so I just said I didn't remember." She bit her bottom lip, and Sam leaned forward in his chair. He let his eyes bore directly into hers for a moment, but said nothing. "Okay, but it was later. My sister knew the guy who got killed, and I called her and was telling her about how the cops were asking me if I had seen this lady, and she told me that they took that lady to jail. She said the smart thing for me to do was stick to my story, because if I changed it, I might get in trouble."

Sam watched her closely, and saw no sign that she was being dishonest. "I can see how she might have thought she was giving you the best advice," he said, "but, Brittany, if you had just admitted that you saw the woman with the wild hair, the police wouldn't have wasted their time arresting the wrong person. That guy was killed less than fifteen minutes before she got back there after leaving here, but even to drive from there to here and back and stopping to buy a coffee takes over forty-five minutes. That means she couldn't possibly have killed him and then come here and made it back when she did."

The tears were flowing freely by the time he finished speaking, and she had grabbed a napkin and was wringing it between her hands. "I didn't mean to do anything wrong," Brittany said. "I mean, the cops arrested her, so I figured she must've done it. I didn't know it happened while she was here, or I would've said so, I swear I would have."

Sam nodded. "At least you're willing to be honest now," he said. "I'm going to have to call Detective Parks, and she'll probably want me to bring you down now. I'm going to tell her that you called me, and said you suddenly remembered seeing her. Okay? That way it makes it sound like you really just wanted to do the right thing, all along, and you won't get in any trouble. That okay with you?"

Tears still streaming, Brittany nodded furiously. "Oh, yes, thank you, thank you," she said. "Really, I didn't mean to do anything wrong, I swear I didn't."

Sam reached across the table and patted her hand. "I know, Brittany," he said. He took out his phone and dialed Karen's number. She answered on the second ring.

"Karen, it's Sam. Listen, I got a call a little bit ago from the girl who works at that coffee shop, the one Candy said she went to that morning? She called me to tell me that she was thinking about it, and she suddenly remembered seeing somebody with multicolored hair that morning. I came down and showed her a picture of Candy on my phone, and she said that's definitely her."

Karen let out a sigh. "Well, hell," she said. "That will help your client, but is there any way she can determine the exact time Candy was there?"

Sam held the phone away for a moment and looked at Brittany. "Brittany, can you tell me what time that lady was here Sunday morning?"

Brittany looked at him for a moment, then held up a finger and jumped up out of her chair. She ran over to the counter and pushed the other girl away from the register for a moment. She tapped a number of keys, and a long strip of paper printed out. She tore it off and hurried back over to Sam.

Brittany laid the paper on the table and ran her finger down a list of transactions, suddenly pointing at one of them. "When I remembered her hair, I remembered that she got a Super Size Hazelnut Mocha and a cheesecake brownie, the one with the cheesecake-flavored frosting. That's this one right here, and look at the time-stamp on it." She took a pen from a pocket and circled the items.

Sam looked, then put the phone back up to his face. "Karen, what time did Charlie call 911 that morning?"

"Just a moment," Karen said, and he could hear her flipping through papers. "That call came in at 9:57 AM."

"And what time have you got down for the probable time of death?"

"Well, Charlie said he found his dad about three minutes after he heard the scream, and he called 911 within a minute or two after that. Why?"

"Because Candy was sitting at the drive-through

window at this coffee shop at the exact moment you figure Carlos was killed. Brittany just got a printout from Sunday morning, and she remembers now what Candy bought. I'm looking at the transaction report, and it shows that she paid for her coffee at exactly 9:52 AM. There's no possible way she could have killed Carlos and made it here in less than a minute, it's a twenty-minute drive."

He could hear Karen groan. "You're killing me, Sam. Can you get that girl down here to make a statement? And bring that printout with her, okay?"

"We'll be there within half an hour," Sam said. "You can go ahead and start the paperwork to get Candy released, because this proves she has an airtight alibi."

"Fine, I'll get it started. You get her down here, and then you get your ass out there and find the real killer for me. That's the least you can do, since you're throwing all this egg on my face."

Sam nodded into the phone, grinning as he remembered that Karen could not see him. "That's my plan," he said. He ended the call and looked at Brittany. "We need to tell your boss that you have to leave for an hour or two. I can assure him that it's police business, if you want, so you won't get in trouble."

She nodded, and went into the back for a moment. She came out a minute later to tell him that her boss said it was okay, and Sam led her out to his car.

Getting Brittany's statement took only twenty

minutes, and Karen thanked her for coming in. Sam told the girl he would meet her back at his car, then waited until she had left the office.

"You got the release paperwork started?"

Karen nodded. "Yeah, I did," she said. "I'll take this over to Monica and get her to sign off on it. With this new evidence, she won't have any choice but to release your friend. It'll probably take a few hours, though; nothing happens around here as fast as we'd like it to."

Sam grinned as he got to his feet. "Isn't that the truth? I'll call her boyfriend and let him know to be waiting. He'll probably go to the jail and just sit in the lobby and wait there."

"As long as he doesn't come down here and wait," Karen said with a grimace. "He's been calling me at least three times a day, and it's driving me crazy."

"Don't worry, I'll take care of Chris." He turned and started toward the door, but then stopped and looked back at Karen. "Incidentally, don't get too excited about going after Randy Whitaker just yet. Would you believe he had the guts to come and face me today? Never even tried to deny what he does, just told me flat out that we'd never find a prosecutor who would touch him."

Karen looked at him for a moment, then threw the pen she was holding onto the desk. "I can believe it," she said. "Like I told you before, there have been rumors about him for years. Nobody has been able to make anything stick so far, so I don't know why I thought we would be able to."

Sam shrugged. "Don't worry, we'll get him. For now, though, he convinced me that he wasn't behind Carlos's killing, so that just leaves me with a few thousand possible suspects."

Karen scowled at him. "By the way, I've got everybody looking for Roland Maxwell. He may not be connected to this murder, but it turns out we want to talk to him about other things. Well, when you figure out who you think might be the killer, you let me know. And if I run up on anyone who looks like a serious possibility for it, I'll tell you. Deal?"

Sam grinned again. "Deal."

15

Sam drove Brittany back to Sammy's, then called Chris Lancaster to let him know the good news. Chris was delighted, and as Sam had predicted, he decided to go down to the jail to wait for Candy's release to be processed. Once that call was finished, Sam decided it was time to check in with Indie.

Indie and Kenzie were out having fun, of course, but Indie had added a feature to Herman that allowed him to send links to his reports straight to her phone. "Sam," she said, "Herman can't find a bank account for Roland Maxwell, anywhere. If he's getting paid the way Carlos was, it must be in cash."

"That figures," Sam said, "but he's been removed from my suspect list, anyway. I was just calling to see how you girls are doing."

Indie laughed. "We're just about to go into Minnie Mouse's house. Don't you wish you were here with us,

Daddy?"

"I sure do," Sam said. "It'd beat the heck out of what I'm doing. You got those guys under control, I take it?"

"Oh, yeah. Kenzie was up till past eleven last night, with all that sugar in her system. I warned them that if they do that again, they are the ones who are going to have to stay up and deal with her. I think that scared them worse than anything else they've ever seen."

Sam chuckled. "That'd do it for me. I have enough trouble keeping up with her when she isn't bouncing off the walls."

"Just a minute, she wants to talk to you." Sam grinned, and suddenly Kenzie's voice came through the phone.

"Daddy! Guess what! I got to drive a car!"

"You did? Wow, that's awesome! Did you run over anybody?"

"No, silly! They got special cars for little kids to drive, and I got to drive one with Mommy and Jennifer."

"That's so cool," Sam said. "If I was there, you could drive me around."

"Okay, she handed the phone back," Indie said. "Kemzie is still in hyper mode, and someone is going to pay for it!" She and Sam talked for another couple of minutes, and then he let her go so that she could keep up with Kenzie. As he hung up the phone, it occurred to him that he was feeling just a little bit lost while they were gone.

Sam continued to drive down the street, and found himself wondering what to do next. His investigation wasn't going anywhere fast, and the only real leads he'd thought he had seemed to be nonexistent.

He thought about Charlie again, and that made him wonder about Carlos's girlfriend. If he could identify her, then it was just possible that she might have some idea who would want him dead. If Sam was right, her husband or boyfriend might be the most logical suspect. Unfortunately, Charlie didn't know who she was, so tracking her down was not going to be easy.

Sam headed back toward Carlos's house. There was always the possibility that one of his neighbors had noticed the woman coming or going. He pulled up there a few moments later and saw that the yellow crime scene tape was still stretched across the front door.

Sam got out of the Corvette, grabbing his cane, and looked around the neighboring houses. The elderly couple was out on their front porch, so he decided to start with them.

Surprisingly, they recognized him instantly. The old man slowly got to his feet and held out a hand, and Sam shook it.

"Mr. Howden, Mrs. Howden," Sam said. "I was wondering if you would mind if I asked you a few more questions."

"Not a bit," the old man said. "Cop a squat, young man." He pointed at another chair on the porch, and

Sam gratefully sat down.

"I appreciate it," he said. "Listen, I was wondering if you ever saw a woman going in and out of Carlos's place. We've been told that he had a girlfriend, but no one seems to know who she was. Any chance you might have seen a woman with long dark hair coming around, or a car that turned up fairly often?"

The old man put his fingers to his chin as he thought, but Mrs. Howden let out a loud snort. Sam looked over at her. "Mrs. Howden? Do you know who she was?"

The elderly lady rocked back and forth for a moment, then looked up at Sam. "I'm not one for gossip, you understand, and what people does is their own business. Just seems to me that they might be just a little bit more discreet, sometimes, but what do I know? I'm just an old woman."

Sam grinned at her. "Sounds like you've got some idea who this lady might be, am I right?"

Mrs. Howden rocked for a few seconds more, then gave a single, curt nod. "Well, they made it obvious, didn't they? Whole neighborhood would know, if people just paid attention to what's going on around them. I mean, her a-traipsing back and forth, all hours of the day and night, just about anytime her husband gone off to work or out doing his own thing."

Sam's eyebrows went up and he leaned closer to the old woman. "Traipsing back and forth? You're saying you think it was one of the people here in the neighborhood?"

"Now, Genevieve," Mr. Howden began, but his wife waved a hand at him to shush him.

"Hush, Kenneth, I'll not be silent. That girl next door," she said. "Sometimes I can't stay asleep, and I get up in the middle of the night. That's one of the things that happens when you get old, you can't sleep right. Anyway, the first time I've seen her going over there, it was about four o'clock in the morning, but that was months ago. Since then, I've seen her cutting across their backyards two or three times a day, it seems like, all hours of the day and night."

Sam glanced over at Carlos's house, then looked back at Mrs. Howden. "How could you see her in the backyard?"

"I didn't see her in the backyard," the old lady said. "I could see her running from behind her house over to the back of his, and if you just look right between their houses, you'll see what I mean."

Sam turned around and looked and, sure enough, he could see about a thirty-foot gap between the two houses. Anyone sitting on the porch or looking out Mrs. Howden's front window would be able to see someone moving from one backyard to the other. The house she was referring to was the one where Sam had talked to the young woman, Marcy. He turned back to the elderly couple.

"So, you think that lady, Marcy, was Carlos's

girlfriend?" Sam asked, and Mrs. Howden gave him a toothless grin.

"One of 'em, anyway. It don't take too many smarts to figure out why a young married lady would be sneaking over to the house where a single young man as good-looking as Carlos lived, now does it?"

Sam grinned back. "No, ma'am," he said, "I don't guess it does. Let me ask you this: Do you know Marcy's husband, by any chance? Would he be the type who might get violent, if he found out Carlos was messing around with his wife?"

Mr. Howden shook his head rather emphatically. "Not Ronnie," he said. "Ronnie Osgood is about as mean as your average caterpillar. Been more than one time I've wondered if he might be a little bit on the funny side, he's such a wimp."

Mrs. Howden was nodding her agreement. "Ronnie wouldn't hurt a fly, even if it was trying to hurt him. He's one of those real soft-spoken-type boys, the kind everybody else pushes around. That wife of his is one of them that pushes him, too. They get into fights now and then, and you can tell who wears the pants in that house, believe you me! It ain't Ronnie Osgood. If he ever caught her sneaking over there, the worst he might do would be to beg her to stop."

"And if she didn't," Mr. Howden interjected, "he'd just put up with it. He never did have any backbone, that boy."

Sam nodded. "Okay, I think I get the picture," he said. "Maybe it's time I go and have another talk with her. If she was that close to Carlos, she might have some idea of who would want him dead."

He thanked the elderly couple and made his way down their front steps and across the street. When he knocked on Marcy's front door, she answered with the same bright smile she'd had on Monday, and Sam noticed her long brown hair. It could easily be the hair Charlie described seeing in the night.

"Oh, hi," she said. "You're the private detective, right?"

"Yeah," Sam said, showing his ID once again. "I had just a couple more quick questions for you. Is now a good time?"

"Oh, sure, ask away," Marcy said. Her smile hadn't wavered, and Sam had to wonder about whether she and Carlos actually had any feelings for one another. She didn't seem to be grieving, that was for sure.

"Marcy, you've been identified as Carlos McAlester's girlfriend. I'm wondering why you didn't mention that fact when I talked to you on Monday."

The smile froze, then slowly fell off of her face. Her eyes were locked on his, as she reached behind herself to pull the front door closed.

"I guess there's no point in trying to deny it, is there?"

Sam shook his head. "Probably not," he said. "You

can talk to me about this, or you can talk to the police, and they're probably going to want to take you downtown for that. Maybe we can avoid some unpleasantness for you, if you're willing to tell me what you know."

She swallowed hard. "It started about a year ago," she said. "I mean, it was just a little flirtation, nothing serious, you know what I mean? Then it got to be a little more flirtation, and finally—well, you can figure it out. It wasn't something I really wanted to do, it just sort of happened. Ronnie, he's gone at work a lot, and he's not the most romantic guy in the world, anyway. I guess I was lonely, but I just hadn't really thought about it up until then. The whole thing got out of hand, and then I didn't know what to do."

Sam looked at her. "So it was still going on?"

She looked down at the ground, and nodded. "Yes, but I had been trying to break it off. If he'd wanted to make it a serious relationship, I probably would have left Ronnie, but I saw other girls going in and out too many times, so I knew he was just using me for sex. I told Carlos I couldn't keep it up, and he'd say he understood, but then he'd call me up when Ronnie was gone, and he'd start talking, and the next thing I knew I was sneaking back over to his place."

Sam nodded. "And were you there on Sunday morning? Charlie thinks he heard you come in."

Marcy crossed her arms across herself and cupped her elbows in her hands. "Earlier that morning, yeah.

Ronnie had a big golf date and left early, and Carlos saw his car pull away. He called and..."

"And you went over, used the key he had given you to unlock the back door and get inside. Right?"

She nodded as if she was ashamed. "Yeah."

"Were you there when his ex-wife showed up?" Sam asked.

Still keeping her eyes lowered, Marcy shook her head. "No, I had already come home. I saw her, though, when she pulled up."

Sam just looked at her for a moment, to see if she would say any more. Finally, he asked, "Marcy, do you have any idea who might have wanted to kill Carlos?"

She finally looked up at him, meeting his eyes with her own. "No, not a clue. It wasn't like we were, you know, a couple. He never told me things about his personal life."

"What about your husband, Ronnie? If he found out, do you think he would do anything like this?"

"No, not Ronnie." She rolled her eyes. "Ronnie—I actually think he knew about it, but he just didn't seem to care. I mean, there were times he came home early, while I was over there. Once he was even in the backyard, and saw me coming out of Carlos's back door. He smiled and asked me how Carlos was doing. I waited all that evening for him to ask what I was doing over there, but he never did. I don't think he knows how to be jealous. If he did, it probably never would have happened at all."

"Let's get back to Sunday morning. Did you happen to see anyone around Carlos's back yard, after his ex left? Right now, we're thinking that someone came in the back door, probably someone who had a key, grabbed the butcher knife and just walked right up to him before stabbing him. Now, that sounds a lot like someone he knew, someone he never would've felt threatened by." He stared hard into her eyes, to see if she had figured out what he was implying.

Unfortunately, Marcy seemed oblivious, at least at first. "No," she said. "After I saw Candy pull up, I sort of did my best not to pay any more attention." She looked at Sam for a moment, and then realization dawned. "Wait a minute, are you saying you think I did it?"

Sam shrugged his shoulders. "Well, I'd have a hard time thinking of anyone else he might trust that much, other than someone he was intimate with. Wouldn't you?"

She started shaking her head emphatically. "No, no way," she said. "I might have wanted out of it, but not that bad."

"Really? You weren't showing any signs of grief when I talked to you on Monday. Seems to me that if you'd had a relationship going on with the guy for a year, you might have been feeling some sort of remorse that he was gone, even if you did want out of it."

Tears suddenly began running from her eyes. "I feel

it," she said. "I just had to keep up an act, so no one would notice. I wouldn't want anyone to think I had anything to do with what happened to him, so I was doing my best to keep it from showing in my face. You can understand that, can't you?"

Sam nodded. "Sure, I can understand it," he said. "I'm not sure how well the police will understand it, or your husband, but I suspect you'll be able to come up with an act for them, too." He handed her his business card, even though he knew he had given her one before. "I'm going to have to report this to Detective Parks, and she will undoubtedly be in touch pretty soon. You might want to be thinking about how you're going to explain this to your husband."

Sam turned and walked away, heading for his car, but then he paused and looked back. "Marcy, do you have a sister?"

She was still standing there, just looking at him. "Yeah," she said. "A younger sister, why?"

"Brittany, right? Works over at Sammy's Coffee Shop?"

Marcy nodded, but didn't say anything.

Sam stood still for a couple of seconds, just looking at her, then turned and went to his car without another word.

He now knew who the mysterious girlfriend was, and her fairly amazing acting ability, plus the fact that she had advised Brittany not to confirm Candy's alibi, had moved her up near the top of his list of suspects. It was a little difficult for him to believe that Marcy could have been as close to Carlos as she claimed without knowing anything at all about his business, and her ability to keep up an innocent act right after he was killed made him wonder if she might have practiced it. Add in the fact that she had helped them to keep Candy's alibi from being confirmed, and he suddenly had a lot of circumstantial evidence.

She had told him she was trying to get out of the relationship. Was it possible that she had actually planned and executed the murder? Sam wondered if she might have simply waited until Candy or another potential murder suspect stopped in and left, then hurried over to do the job quickly and let it be blamed on the visitor.

In the past, he had certainly known both men and women who were capable of such coldhearted planning. Under the right circumstances, any of us, he knew, can be capable of cold-blooded murder. There was little doubt in his mind that any woman could kill, if her motivation was strong enough.

16

Sam decided that it was time for lunch, so he fired up the Corvette and pointed it toward downtown, then took out his phone to call Detective Parks.

"Karen," Sam said when she answered, "I got an ID on McAlester's girlfriend. Her name is Marcy Osgood, she lives next door. I was right about her being married, too."

"Any sense that she might be our killer?" Karen asked.

"I'd put her up pretty high on the list of suspects," Sam said. "She says the affair went on for about a year, and that she'd been trying to get out of it, but Carlos could always talk her into coming back. Could be she decided to take matters into her own hands. She's a cool customer, and if she feels any grief over him, she keeps it hidden well." He decided not to mention her relationship to Brittany just yet, but it could always be brought up later.

"I'm gonna pull her in for questioning. What about her husband, could be we're dealing with jealous rage, maybe?"

"Everyone I talked to seems to think her husband is too meek to hurt anyone, but you and I both know that anyone can snap. My gut says it isn't him, but that doesn't mean I would leave him out of the questioning."

Sam took a right onto Fifth Avenue, and a quick glance in his rearview mirror showed the car behind making the same turn. He had vaguely noticed it back there when he had pulled away from Marcy's place, and it struck him as a little odd that it would be going the same way he was.

"Sorry? I missed that," Sam said to Karen, who had spoken.

"I just said we'll bring him in and talk with him, too. Your gut tends to be pretty right on, but we can't afford to leave any possible suspects out of the investigation. I'll let you know if I come up with anything, and I'd appreciate it if you'd do the same for me. And now that I think of it, aren't you done with this case? You already cleared your client. Surely they're not going to pay you to keep looking for the killer, now that she's in the clear, are they?"

Sam laughed. "This was a pro bono case," he said. "Our band isn't rich enough that they could afford to pay me. I just sort of need to know who killed Carlos for my own satisfaction, now. Besides, Chris had to give all his money to Candy's lawyer."

"Poor guy," Karen said. "Good luck with getting any of that money back. Lawyers can hold on to money better than anybody else in the world."

"Yeah, well, I would have hired a lawyer, too. The case looked pretty bad for her when I started on this, and I wouldn't have taken any bets on whether she could get out of it or not."

"I gotcha. Well, listen, I'm going to jump on this. I'll let you know how it goes."

"Same here," Sam said, and then he ended the call. The powder blue Mustang was still behind him, and he changed lanes to get ready for another turn, this time onto Broadway. The Mustang moved over behind him, and when he turned right, it followed again.

Peering hard into his rearview mirror, Sam tried to figure out who might be driving the car, but its blacked-out windows made it too dark in the car's cabin to get any kind of look at the driver. He thought it was a woman, and wondered for a moment if it could be Marcy, but her car had still been in her driveway when he'd left, and it wasn't a Mustang.

Sam weaved in and out of traffic for a few minutes, and the Mustang stayed within a few car lengths of him. He waited until the last possible moment to make his next turn, onto West Seventeenth Avenue, then whipped around the corner without even touching his turn signal.

The Mustang came around behind him, its own signal blinking. There was no doubt that Sam was being followed, and the hairs on the back of his neck began to rise. Just ahead, he saw Steuben's restaurant, and deliberately fishtailed into the parking lot. He spun the car around as quickly as he could and backed it into a parking slot.

The Mustang turned in more sedately, and Sam watched as it motored slowly to where he was parked. There were no empty spaces nearby, but the car suddenly stopped right in front of the Corvette. It just sat there for a few seconds, and Sam let his hand rest on the grip of his pistol.

The driver window of the Mustang suddenly powered down, and Sam found himself looking into the face of Jackie Porter, the CSI tech. She was looking directly at him and smiling, so Sam popped his door open and climbed slowly out of the Corvette.

"Did I spook ya?" Jackie asked.

"Maybe just a little bit," Sam said. "When you're trying to track down a murder suspect and someone starts following you through the city, it does tend to make you just a little bit nervous. What are you doing, tailing an old geezer like me?"

Jackie laughed. "I was actually going back to McAlester's house to take a look at a couple of things that were unclear, when I spotted you driving away. I just figured I'd catch up with you at your next stop and see if you had any new brilliant epiphanies about the case."

Sam grinned. "Brilliant epiphanies aren't something that tend to happen to me very often," he said. "Actually, I'm about to go have lunch. Care to join me? Maybe if we brainstorm a bit together, we'll come up with something."

"Sure," Jackie said. "Just let me park this behemoth, and I'll meet you at the door."

Sam nodded, and made his way toward the front door of the restaurant. The place was known for its incredible food, and was a highly popular tourist destination. Fortunately, Sam knew just about everyone who worked there, so it wasn't hard for him to get a table. He held up two fingers to the hostess, and a moment later one of the waiters came to show him the way. Jackie came jogging up just then, and simply followed them inside.

The waiter took their drink orders as he seated them and gave them menus to look over, and both of them were ready to order by the time he came back. Sam went for the cheesesteak sandwich, and after asking his opinion of it, Jackie opted for the same.

"So what were you looking for at McAlester's place?" Sam asked when they were alone.

Jackie grinned. "You got me to thinking about just how odd it was, the way McAlester was laid out. It was almost like somebody positioned him, but that should have left smears in the bloodstains and there weren't any.

On top of that, I wanted to find out just how easy it would be for someone to come in the back door without being seen. I took a quick glance the other day, after you left, and there are enough garages and hedges and such back along the alley so that only one of his immediate neighbors might have seen whoever came in that way. I know you talked to them; did anyone mention seeing someone in the backyard?"

Sam nodded. "Old couple across the street," he said. "They saw the neighbor, Marcy Osgood, slipping between the two houses, going from her own backyard into his. Karen is talking to her today, I think. Right now, she's pretty high on the suspect list."

Jackie's eyebrows went up. "Oh, really? I met her the other day, right after you left. She was out in her front yard as I was going to the van and said hello. She didn't act like someone who cared much about him."

"No, she made it pretty clear that it was just a sexual thing. She implied that if Carlos had ever wanted it to be more, she might have been willing to explore the possibility, but she said he was only using her. She claims she wanted out of the relationship, but said he could always talk her into coming back. If she really wanted out and felt she just didn't have the willpower to stop, that could be motive for murder."

"True," Jackie mused. "Was she the only one they ever saw going in there?"

Sam shrugged. "The old lady might have implied that

there were others, but I guess it wasn't anyone she knew. I didn't actually think to ask for more information, and now that I think about it, I should have. I'll run back over there this afternoon, see if she might have gotten a description of any of the others."

"Well, if she had seen somebody going in there regularly, she probably would've mentioned that, don't you think?"

"Yeah, probably," Sam said, "but you can never be sure. It can't hurt to run back by."

"I guess not. Hey, I heard you got your bass player girl out of this mess. How'd that happen, if you don't mind my asking?"

"I got to thinking about the girl at the coffee shop, the one who said she didn't remember Candy being there. When I went in to show her Candy's picture, she didn't want to look me in the eye when she insisted she'd never seen her before. That left me thinking that she was lying, even though I couldn't figure out why she would want to. Turns out she said it when the cops first called her just because she didn't want to get involved, but then she said her sister advised her not to say anything, because changing her story might get her into trouble. With a little nudge from me, she owned up and then wanted to be helpful. She remembered exactly what Candy had ordered and found the cash register printout that showed the time she was there. That proved Candy couldn't possibly have killed Carlos, because she would've been in the drive-through line at Sammy's at the time. Oh, and the sister? The one who told her to keep her mouth shut? Marcy Osgood."

Jackie nodded appreciatively. "Good work there, Mr. Private Investigator. So now the cops have to find the real killer, right? You're not working on that, now, are you?"

Sam shrugged again. "Just for myself," he said. "Whoever did it is probably the person who sent me this." Sam pulled out the photo of Kenzie with the crosshairs and handed it to Jackie. She took it carefully, as if afraid of getting her fingerprints on it.

"Oh, my God, Sam," she said. "Is that your little girl?"

Sam nodded. "That's McKenzie, and that picture was taken in our backyard. Somebody snapped it, printed it out, drew the crosshairs on it and stuffed it in an envelope addressed to my wife, Indie. She found it in our mailbox, but it didn't have stamps on it and didn't come through the mail. I guess they thought that would make me back off."

Jackie looked up from the picture. "Where is your family now? Surely you got them put away safe, right?"

"Damn right," Sam said. "Sometimes it's nice to have powerful people owe you a favor. My wife and daughter are enjoying a vacation in Orlando right now, with enough security on them to take care of a small army. They're safe, and I dare whoever did this to try coming after me."

He took the photo back from Jackie and slipped it back into his pocket. She shook her head, as if stunned that anyone would try such a stunt. "Well, maybe now that you got your client cleared, the real killer will just leave you alone."

"I hope not," Sam said. "Whoever killed Carlos McAlester did it while his eight-year-old son was in the house, and it was the boy who found him dead. I want to nail whoever did this, for that kid's sake."

"Yeah, that was pretty rotten. Maybe it will turn out to be the neighbor lady, maybe she didn't even know the boy was there."

"I don't know," Sam said. "I just want to get to the bottom of it, or help the cops get there."

Sam's phone rang suddenly, and he pulled it out to look at the caller ID. His eyes went wide when he saw that it was his mother calling, because she almost never called him. "Mom?"

"Sam, it's Kim, I don't know what's gotten into her," his mother said. "It's that ghost of hers, she's gone into that trance thing again. She says the ghost wants to talk to you, right now."

"Oh, dear Lord," Sam said. "Okay, fine, put her—put *it* on."

"Samuel?" The voice that came through the phone didn't sound like Kim at all, but had a deeper, more masculine quality and a Southerner's accent. "I do hope you'll forgive me, but my message to you is urgent, and I could not wait for this dear lady to gain the courage to speak to you about it."

Sam gave a sigh, and tried to avoid the piercing look Jackie was casting his way. "What is it, Beauregard?"

"You need to know that the man who died was not the killer's first victim, and that this murderer will strike again. You already know the killer, and if you can deduce who it is, you can save lives."

Sam's eyes went wide, and he threw a hand to his forehead. "Beauregard, can't you just give me the name? Tell me who it is, so I can stop it?"

"I don't have the name, Samuel," the eerie voice said. "I cannot choose the knowledge that comes to me, I can only pass on those parts of it that may pertain to you." Suddenly Sam heard coughing, and then he heard his mother-in-law's voice. "Grace? Who's on the phone? Hello?"

"It's me, Kim, it's Sam. Apparently Beauregard wanted to tell me something, so he decided to take over driving for a bit."

"Beauregard? Was it about the case you're working on? He's been telling me I needed to call you, but I've been busy."

Sam rolled his eyes. "Yeah, well, I guess Beauregard got tired of waiting for you to not be busy. If he asks, I got the message and I'm doing all I can with it."

Sam ended the call, and then allowed himself to look

at Jackie. "Do me a favor," he said. "Don't even ask."

Jackie's eyes were very wide, but she didn't say a word for a long moment or two. Finally, Sam could tell that she'd held it back as long as she could. "Beauregard? Who on earth is Beauregard?"

Sam shook his head. "As crazy as it sounds, Beauregard seems to be an old Confederate war ghost. He and my mother-in-law are pretty chummy, and sometimes he sends me messages. The bad part is that, so far, he's never been wrong and he's saved my life on more than one occasion."

Jackie stared at him. "I believe in ghosts," she said. "I've seen them, more than once at a crime scene." She shrugged. "I haven't ever had one of them talk to me, or tell me who killed them, but I've seen them."

"Okay, can we just not make ghosts a topic of conversation? It's really not something I want to talk about right now."

"But what did the ghost say? Did he tell you who the killer is?"

Sam shook his head. "No," he said. "According to Beauregard, I already know the killer, but I have to figure out who it is for myself."

Jackie sat in silence for a moment, then shrugged again. "Well, best of luck, I guess."

17

The food arrived, and they talked about less serious things as they ate. Then Sam got another call. This one was from Karen Parks, asking him to come down to the station and observe her questioning of Marcy Osgood. "I don't want her to see you, you can just watch through the mirror glass, but I want you to let me know if you think she's hiding anything. You've already talked to her, so you might have a better sense of when she's being deceptive."

"No problem," Sam said. "I'm not that far away, I can be there in about fifteen minutes."

Sam traded cell numbers with Jackie, and said goodbye, walked out to his car and headed for the station. Observing an interrogation didn't strike him as something truly productive, but Karen had done him favors in the past, so he didn't want to turn her down. Besides, if Marcy cracked and confessed, Sam wanted to be there to hear it.

As he drove, Sam thought about Beauregard's message. If the old spook was right, then Carlos's killer had struck before. Sam tried to recall any similar killings, but failed. If only Beauregard had been able to give him a lead on what other victims the killer might have had, it could have made figuring out which of his acquaintances he was trying to identify much easier.

Beauregard says I already know the killer, Sam thought to himself, *and the killer has killed before, and will kill again. I guess that's what he meant when he said that if I figure it out, I can save lives. If I can stop him, there won't be any future victims.*

He kept thinking it over all the way to the police station, and was still letting it roll around inside his head as he slipped into the observation room. Marcy and a lawyer—it was Carol Spencer, a lawyer that Sam knew well—were already seated at the table. Karen was in the observation room when Sam entered.

"Okay, I'm going in," she said. "If you hear anything you think I should know about, grab one of the uniforms and tell him to get me."

Sam nodded and Karen left the room, closing the door behind her. It was dark in the observation room, which was what made the one-way glass work. Sam could see through it perfectly, but on Marcy's side it was nothing but a mirror.

Sam saw Karen enter and take a seat. The voices

came through a speaker over his head, picked up by hidden microphones in the room.

"Mrs. Osgood, Ms. Spencer, thank you both for coming down so quickly. I've actually just got a few questions, Mrs. Osgood, regarding your relationship with Carlos McAlester. I've spoken with Sam Prichard, and he has shared with me the things you told him. I just need to get them on record for the police department."

"Okay, I guess," Marcy said. The attorney sat beside her, but didn't say a word.

"All right, Mrs. Osgood, you told Sam Prichard that you and Mr. McAlester had been having an affair for about a year? Is that correct?"

"Well, when I thought about it afterward, it was probably more like maybe a year and a half, or a little less than that. It went on for a while."

"Was it a serious affair? Were you and Mr. McAlester thinking of being together permanently?"

Marcy shook her head. "Oh, no," she said. "It was just a physical thing, just about sex. I don't, um, I don't always get what I need at home. Not that that's an excuse, I don't mean that, I just meant that was why it got started. Carlos was attractive and I was lonely. It just sort of happened."

"So, neither of you ever wanted anything more?"

Marcy glanced at Carol Spencer, but the lawyer simply grinned and nodded. "I probably had fantasies about something more permanent, and if he had ever asked, I probably would've been willing to leave my husband. I'm just being honest, here. It was just wishful thinking on my part, though, and Carlos never brought it up at all. I wasn't the only woman he was having fun with, so I'm sure he didn't want to have to give up his other extracurricular activities."

"And do you know who any of those other women might be?" Karen asked.

Marcy shook her head. "No, I'm afraid I don't. There was one girl I've seen going in his back door a couple of times, but all I can tell you is that she had black hair, and she was taller than me, too. I have no idea who she was."

Karen nodded, and went on with her questioning. Marcy told her basically the same things she had said to Sam, and he didn't pick up on anything that might have indicated she was being deceptive. The entire interrogation took only about an hour, and then Marcy was allowed to leave.

Karen stepped back into the observation room. "Any comments?" she asked Sam.

Sam shook his head. "No, her story didn't change much. She offered you the information that the affair lasted longer than she had first told me, but that might've simply been because I caught her off guard when I asked about it. To be honest, she's pretty believable. I'd have to say I'm moving her down my list a little bit. Now if only I knew who's in the slots above her, maybe I'd have something."

Karen sighed heavily. "You don't have any leads? Granted, this case isn't high priority, but it irks me to have a killer running loose when we don't have a clue who it might be."

Sam hesitated for a second, and then gave a sigh of his own. "I got—well, let's call it an anonymous tip a little while ago. Somebody told me that Carlos's killer has killed before, and implied that it was more than once. They also said he's going to kill again, and if I can figure out who it is, I might save lives."

Karen just looked at him for a moment. "Are we talking about a serial killer, here? I wonder what would have put McAlester on a serial killer's hit list."

Sam shook his head. "I don't know," he said. "I've tried to think of any other murders that might fit the same MO, but I've drawn a blank. Any ideas?"

"No, but let's go check the computer. Maybe we'll turn something up and generate a lead." She turned and walked out of the room, and Sam followed her to her office.

She scanned through all of the open cases involving stabbings, but didn't find anything that seemed genuinely similar. In order to look at them more closely, she printed the crime scene reports on about a dozen of them, handing half of them to Sam to go through while she looked through the rest.

Fifteen minutes later, they put them all back in the

stack. Neither had noticed anything that might create a pattern, so Sam was more confused than ever.

"How sure are you of your tipster?" Karen asked, and Sam grimaced.

"I can tell you that he's never been wrong before, at least not as long as I've known him," he said. "If he says this killer has killed before, I'm going to tend to believe it."

Karen snorted. "I wish I had an informant I trusted that much. All the ones I know spend more time trying to shake me down for money than giving me information I can actually count on." She picked up the stack again. "Well, let's look through these one more time. I don't have any other options to go on."

This time she gave Sam the stack she had looked through before, while she took his. Still, neither of them saw any pattern in the way the killings had been carried out. There was nothing in any of them to indicate that more than one of them might have been the work of a single individual.

"There just isn't anything here, Karen," Sam said. "If we're dealing with a serial killer, then it's one who's smart enough not to use the same technique twice."

Karen nodded her head. "True," she said. "And to be honest, if there was a pattern in any of these, I'm pretty sure CSI would've spotted it. Most of these were handled by Jackie Porter, and she's one of the best crime scene techs we've ever had. If there was a pattern, I think she would've noticed it."

Sam nodded. "Yeah, she's good. I actually got to work with her a bit the other day, at the McAlester house." When he saw Karen's face, he held up both hands to ward off the reaming he knew was about to come. "Relax, relax, she made me put on the booties and gloves, and wouldn't let me touch anything. I didn't contaminate the crime scene, I promise you."

"I didn't figure you would," Karen said, "but there are rules about letting civilians into a crime scene. I won't say anything this time, and I guess I do trust Jackie's judgment. Still, you might have mentioned that before."

Sam looked at her quizzically. "Wait a minute, I thought Jackie told you. It was just before she called to tell you that little Charlie couldn't possibly have heard his father scream. I was the one who tested that with her, I was in Charlie's room while she screamed in the living room to see if I could hear her."

Karen shrugged. "She knows the rules, she probably didn't mention you because she didn't want to get herself in trouble. Anyway, it's water under the bridge now. I just want to figure out what it is your informant is trying to tell us, or tell you. How do we tie this killing to others in the past?"

"I wish I knew. It would make my life a lot easier right now. So now, we've got to figure out who this is. My informant says this killer isn't done, and I don't want any other people dying because we failed to do our jobs."

Karen agreed, and Sam got up to leave the office. He made his way to the station and out the door, and had almost made it to his car when his phone rang again. The caller ID said it was his mother's number once more, and he groaned.

"Yes?"

"Sam, it's Mom. That stupid freaking ghost is at it again! Hang on a second, he wants to talk to you."

Sam waited, and then that strange voice came through the phone. "Samuel, you are running out of time. You have to hurry, because they're too old. The shock alone could kill them."

Sam's eyes went wide. "What? Who are you talking about? Who's too old?"

"What?" It was his mother-in-law's voice once again, without the strange timbre that marked a visit from Beauregard. "Sam? Oh no, is he up to it again?"

"Yeah, he is! He said something about me running out of time, and that someone is too old. Any idea what he's talking about?"

"No, Sam, I'm sorry. He probably doesn't know any more than that himself, he doesn't always get things clear. I'm sorry, but if he tells me anything more, I'll call you right away."

"Yeah," Sam said bitterly, "you do that. Meanwhile, I got to try to figure out who is about to die from shock!"

Sam ended the call and got behind the wheel, his mind racing in an attempt to make sense of the cryptic message. He quickly recalled everything Beauregard had told him, and tried to make it all fit together like pieces of a puzzle.

I already know the killer, even though I don't know who it is, he thought. *The killer has killed before, and is going to kill again unless I stop him. And I have to hurry, because I'm running out of time, and somebody is too old...*

Sam suddenly froze. "Too old?" Sam said aloud. He fired up the big engine and shoved the shifter into first gear. His tires left black marks on the parking lot of the police station as he roared out onto the street. There was only one possible connection to this case where the words "too old" might come into play.

Sam drove like a maniac, the Corvette sliding around corners at more than fifty miles an hour, then hitting a hundred and twenty on the straightaways. He was weaving in and out of traffic like a formula race driver, and trying to dial his phone at the same time.

Karen didn't answer until the fourth ring. "Sam? What..."

"The Howdens!" Sam shouted into the phone. "They're the old couple who lived across the street from Carlos's house! I think something is about to happen to them, can you get any units down there right away?"

"I'm on it," Karen yelled back, and the phone went dead.

Sam didn't slow down. It was almost a half hour drive

from the station to the Howden residence normally, but Sam made it in just over ten minutes. He slid to a stop at the curb in front of their house and all but flew out of the car.

It was midafternoon, but the old couple was not on their front porch as they usually were. Sam rushed as quickly as he could up the walk and the steps, and then pounded on the door. "Mr. Howden? Mrs. Howden? It's Sam Prichard, are you here?"

From somewhere inside the house, Sam heard a muffled scream, and he yanked the storm door open. He tried the knob but found it locked, so he threw himself against the front door as hard as he could. It took three tries, but finally he broke the lock and the door flew open. "Mr. Howden? Where are you?"

There was no screen, this time, but he heard a groan toward the back of the house. He snatched his Glock from its holster as he made a hobbling run across the living room and down the hallway. There were several doors, and he tried each of them with his left hand, the gun gripped tightly in his right.

Each of them seemed to lead to an empty room, and Sam moved as quickly as he could to the next each time. He was about to open the last door in the hallway when he heard the groan again. It was coming from behind the door, so he braced his back against the wall beside it and reached for the knob to throw it open.

Nothing happened, so he peeked around the

doorframe. Mr. Howden was lying on a bed, and he had obviously been struck in the face. There was blood around his mouth and nose, but he was alert and conscious, and holding out a hand toward Sam. Sam stepped inside, checked behind the door and in the closet, then turned to the old man.

Mr. Howden had a frantic look on his face. "She—she..."

"Where is your wife, Mr. Howden? Where is she?" Sam asked, and the old man pointed toward the back wall. Sam spun around to look, but there was nothing there except the closet he had already checked. He looked back at the old man.

"Out...back," the old fellow gasped out. "Shed..."

"Okay, stay right here, I'm going to go find her. I'll be back, just wait." Sam stepped back into the hall and yanked open a door that led into the kitchen. He had ignored that room before, because he didn't see anyone in it, but now he hurried across it to the back door that led into the rear yard.

There was a shed in the yard, all right, and Sam hurried out toward it, his gun held at the ready. He listened at the door of the shed for a moment, then snatched it open.

Mrs. Howden was lying on the floor of the shed, just in front of a potting bench. A very large clay pot had been shattered over her head, and she was bleeding profusely. Sam quickly felt for a pulse and found it, then whipped out his phone and called 911. As he told the dispatch operator to send an ambulance to the address, he heard sirens coming down the street and knew that Karen's uniform patrols had arrived.

A half-dozen officers stormed the house, and two ran into the backyard. Sam yelled for help, and one of the officers hurried over to the shed. Between the two of them, they managed to move the shattered flowerpot fragments away from the old woman, and Sam held onto her hand until the paramedics arrived six minutes later.

“She was in pretty rough shape,” one of them said to Sam as they loaded her into an ambulance. “As bad as she's hurt, and as hot as it was in that shed, it's a wonder she's even alive at all. We got her stable at the moment, and we'll get her to the hospital ASAP.”

“What about her husband, in the house? He was hurt, too.”

“Yes, but not as badly as his wife. We got another ambulance on the way right now, they'll take care of him.” The paramedic climbed into the ambulance and shut the door behind him, leaving Sam standing there.

Sam turned and hobbled back into the house, and went to the bedroom where Mr. Howden was still lying on the bed. One of the officers had gotten a wet cloth and wiped some of the blood from his face, and it looked to Sam like he might have a broken nose, but probably nothing more serious than that.

“Mr. Howden, can you talk?” Sam asked, and the

old man nodded vigorously.

"I got a split lip and a sore nose, but I can talk. Did you get her?"

Sam nodded. "Yes, your wife is on the way to the hospital. She's hurt, but I got a feeling she's a tough old bird, and I think she'll be back to keep you in line."

The old man shook his head. "I know she'll be okay, you can't kill that old broad," he said. "I mean the bitch who did this! Did you get her?"

Sam's eyes went wide. "You're saying a woman did this to you? Do you know who it was?"

Mr. Howden shook his head. "I never seen her before, but Genevieve said she was one of the women who used to go over to see Carlos. I couldn't see her face, because she had one of them stockings down over it, but she was a real tall gal with black hair. I know that, because some of it was hanging out at the back. She said we were too nosy, and she had to shut us up. She hit me and dragged me back here, and wanted to know where Genevieve was. I said I didn't know, but then she heard Gen calling me from the shed." Tears were coming from his eyes. "She went out there to put some flowers in the pot, she wanted to put them over in front of Carlos's house. What did we ever do to this woman?"

Sam looked down at where the old man lay, his face swollen and bloodied and his eyes filled with tears for his wife. "You told me something that she didn't want me to know," he said. "And now you've told me exactly who

I'm looking for."

18

The second ambulance arrived a few moments later, and Sam got out of the way so they could help the old man. He walked out the front door of the house, headed across the street to where the Osgoods lived, and knocked. A short, thin man opened the door.

"You must be Ronnie," Sam said. "I'm Sam Prichard, a private investigator. Are you folks okay over here?"

Ronnie shrugged. "Well, it's not every day you find out your wife has been cheating on you with the guy who got murdered next door, but I guess we're coping. Is there something I can do for you?"

Sam nodded. "Yes. Keep your doors locked and stay inside for a bit. The person who killed Carlos is apparently trying to eliminate any possible witnesses. The old couple across the street was attacked just a short time ago, and since your wife and Carlos were involved, she might be considered another potential risk. Has anyone come around here, asking questions today?"

"Only the police," Ronnie said. "Do they know who killed Carlos yet? I might want to send the guy a thank you card."

Sam glared at him. "Mr. Osgood, what you need to do is try to figure out how to save your marriage. And if anyone comes around here acting suspicious, especially a tall woman, you call the police just as fast as you can."

Sam turned around and walked away, heading back to his car. He took out his phone and called Karen as he climbed inside.

"Karen, I know who it is, but you're going to have a hard time believing me. It's Jackie Porter. I don't have a clue why, yet, but she's the only person who knew that it was the Howdens who tipped me off to Marcy, and said they had seen other women at Carlos's place. They've been attacked, and Mr. Howden says it was a woman who is taller than me and has long black hair. Two plus two makes four, even in this messed-up world."

Karen was quiet for a moment, but then she said, "Remember all those crime scene reports we went through? Every single one of them was prepared by Jackie. If there were any similarities in those cases, who better to cover them up than the crime scene technician handling the case? Sam, how sure are you of this? I'll stick my neck out with you, but you'd better be able to back it up or we're both likely to lose our heads."

"I'm certain," Sam said. "Still, what kind of motive could she possibly have had? Jackie is one of the best CSIs in the business, what would make her turn to murder?"

"Tell you what," Karen said. "We'll ask her that once we've caught her. I'm going to give her a call and ask her to come down and go over the McAlester report with me. If she isn't aware that you're on to her, she'll probably try to act like there's nothing out of the ordinary."

"Good," Sam said. "I'm on my way there."

He cut the call and fired up the Corvette, then started back toward the police station. As he drove, he was wracking his brain, trying to figure out any possible motive for Jackie to kill Carlos.

Suddenly, it hit him—the pieces started to fall into place. Whitaker had told him that Carlos had the ability to make evidence disappear, and Marcy told Karen that she had seen a tall woman with black hair going in and out of Carlos's home. If Carlos and Jackie were involved, it was quite possible that he convinced her to tamper with evidence from time to time; it would be easy for her, with her position in the department. Almost every kind of physical evidence from any type of case passed through her office.

When he added in the fact that only Jackie knew about the Howdens filling him in on Marcy, she was the only possible person who could want them silenced. She would need to be sure they couldn't tell anyone about her own visits to Carlos, because that would automatically put her on the suspect list.

Suddenly, Sam thought it made sense that she hadn't caught on at the crime scene. She should have realized on her own that Carlos knew and trusted his attacker, and would have already written that into her report, except that she needed to reinforce the police perception that Candy was the killer. Sam's fortuitous appearance had thrown a monkey wrench into her plans, which explained why she tracked him down earlier; she was trying to find out if he was getting any closer to connecting her to the crime.

His phone rang, and it was Karen calling. "Sam, she's not answering her phone. Think about it, is there any way she could know you're onto her yet?"

Sam took a deep breath. "I don't know whether she was still around the Howden house when I got there or not," he said. "It's quite possible she was still there, and saw me come roaring in. On the other hand, she's smart, and she'd know that Mr. Howden was going to describe her. With everything I've got, she might expect me to put it together."

"Then she's bolting," Karen said. "I'm sending some plainclothes out to her place now, to see if they see any sign of her. You got any other ideas where we might look?"

Sam thought for a moment. "I don't know her that

well," he said. "She had a new partner, a guy named Ned, the other day. See if you can find out how to reach him. Jackie tends to fraternize, or at least she did back when I was in homicide. Some of the people she worked with should know more about her."

"Gotcha, I'll get on that." The phone went dead again.

Sam kept going over the little details of the case, trying to think of anything that might give him a clue to what was going on in Jackie's mind. She had been an excellent CSI, and there were literally dozens of men and women sitting in prison because of evidence she had uncovered that everyone else had missed. Now, all of those cases would be called into question. If she were connected to Carlos, and he was known for being able to make evidence vanish, then she had to be an accomplice.

Still, it's a big leap from tampering with evidence to murder. Sam couldn't imagine any circumstance that would take a brilliant CSI scientist and turn her into a killer.

His phone rang again, and this time the caller ID was blocked. He answered warily. "Hello?"

"You seem to have set off a beehive," said a voice, and Sam recognized it as Randall Whitaker. "I'm hearing rumors that McAlester's killer has been identified, and it's got an awful lot of people upset. Care to tell me who it is?"

Sam thought for a moment, and decided that having Whitaker on his side could come in handy sometime, and would keep the man from realizing just how determined Sam was to bring him to justice. "Her name is Jackie Porter, and she's a crime scene technician for the Denver PD. You said Carlos was able to make evidence disappear? Well, I'm pretty sure we know how, now. I don't know what the connection between Carlos and Jackie was, yet, but when I put the pieces together, they all add up to her."

Whitaker whistled. "No joke? I wonder why she killed him?"

Sam shrugged, even though Whitaker couldn't see him. "That's the thing we need to find out, or one of them. It turns out she may have been responsible for other murders in the past, and with her position, she could cover it up and let it remain unsolved, or let someone else take the fall. I'm working with the police on this, and we're trying to get enough pieces to put this puzzle together."

"Do you think it has any connection to me? I mean, could she have wanted revenge over something I arranged?"

"Still no clue. We made a deal, though, so if I find out you'll be the first to know."

Whitaker was satisfied, and ended the call only a moment later after promising that Sam would not regret his cooperation. Sam grimaced as he put the phone back into his pocket, but it rang before he could even let go of it. He snatched it back out and shoved it to his ear. "Prichard," he said.

It was Karen Parks again. "Sam, Jackie's partner Ned seems to be missing. The lab says he got a phone call about an hour and a half ago, and left suddenly. No one knows who the call was from, but we called his home, and his father says he isn't there and has no idea where he could be."

Sam shook his head in frustration. "They could be working together," he said, "or she might have called him out on a pretext. I think you should get an APB out on both of their personal vehicles, and make sure the CSI van is accounted for."

"What, do you think I'm stupid? Already did that. The van is at the lab, right where it's supposed to be. Jackie's car is a brand-new Mustang, and Ned Jacobson drives a 2014 Challenger. Sam, if she's running, she can be just about anywhere within a hundred miles right now."

"No, she hasn't gotten that far. When I got to Mr. Howden, she had only been out of the house for a short time. Even if she saw me show up there and took off, she's only had about a twenty-minute head start. It wouldn't be that easy for her to get out of town without somebody on our side spotting her."

"Fine, I'll keep you posted. If you think of anything, you let me know."

Sam was quivering with frustration, kicking himself for not having caught on sooner. Still, he knew that it wasn't until Mr. Howden's description that all the pieces suddenly fell into place. He tried to think of anything that would lead him to Jackie now, but he had no clue what her plans were.

Sam started trying to think like a fleeing killer, planning how he would escape the city without running across police officers who might be looking for him. There were a number of roads that went out into the countryside, but there was little doubt they would be heavily patrolled at the moment. If there was one thing a cop couldn't stand, it was to see one of their own literally fleeing from justice. Every cop on duty would be watching for any sign of Jackie, so it wasn't likely she could take any of the more common routes.

That being the case, she would certainly be driving a different vehicle than usual, something that wouldn't be noticed as readily as her own. With her skills, she would have no trouble hotwiring a vehicle, but that would limit her to older cars that didn't require a key to unlock the steering or transmission.

In today's modern automotive world, however, there are a lot of new cars that don't require a key at all. All you need is a key fob in your pocket, and you can simply push a button to start the car. That's a wonderful thing, but it's also enabled high-tech car thieves to run off with your fancy new vehicle. A simple device, designed to allow a dealership or locksmith to create a new key fob if your original is lost, can be plugged into a slot in your car to override that system. You simply plug it in, push the button and the car starts, allowing you to drive away without anyone knowing the car is stolen.

As a crime scene technician, Jackie would know about such devices and even have access to them. She could literally be in any of several dozen brand-new vehicles that were cruising around him at that moment, and he would never know.

But that didn't mean she couldn't be found. Sam yanked his phone out of his pocket again and called his wife.

"Hey, baby," Indie said as she answered.

"Indie, is there any possibility you're close to your computer?"

"Oh, yeah," she said. "We've been out having fun, but now were back at the hotel to rest up before dinner. What do you need?"

Sam grinned. "I need you to find a cell phone for me." He gave her Jackie's number, and could hear her typing it into Herman's search fields. "How long do you think it will take to get a GPS location on her?"

"If that's all you need, I should be able to get it within a few minutes. Hang on, let me turn Herman loose."

While Herman started searching for Jackie's phone, Indie filled Sam in on the day she and Kenzie had had, running wild through parts of Disney World that she hadn't even known existed until that day. They chatted for a few minutes, and then Herman went *ding*!

"Okay, I've got it," Indie said. "That phone is heading south on 85, just about to cross Oxford. That help anything?"

Sam tapped the speaker button on his phone and dropped it into his shirt pocket, then looked around for a split second. Realizing where he was, he grabbed the shifter and downshifted to second gear as he yanked the wheel to the left and spun the car around. "It sure does," he yelled. "Now just stay with me and help me zero in on the car it's riding in."

Sam was on Broadway just north of Oxford, so he floored the car and took the right turn onto Oxford at almost 60 miles an hour. Cars were honking and drivers were making hand gestures, but Sam didn't take his eyes off the road. Just over two minutes later, he swung left onto 85.

"Okay," he said to Indie, "I just turned onto 85 from Oxford, going south. How far ahead of me?"

"Um, it's just about to pass Belleview. Still going south, probably doing about fifty, fifty-five miles an hour."

Sam shifted back into high gear and floored the accelerator again, watching his speedometer read higher and higher. He was doing a hundred and twenty, and still climbing. The big four twenty-seven under the hood was roaring, and Sam actually thought he could hear a note of relief in the loud exhaust. The car had been built to run like this, but it wasn't something he could do often.

Sam held the throttle steady when he made it to a hundred and forty. There weren't a lot of intersections on that stretch, so he wasn't running a great risk of someone pulling out in front of him. "How far ahead now?"

"It's halfway between Belleview and Bowles," Indie said. "Where are you?"

"Sign says Belleview is a two miles ahead," Sam said.

"Then you're about a three miles behind the car with that phone. Sam, who are you chasing?"

"Remember I told you about Jackie, my old friend in the CSI lab? Guess who turned out to be the killer in this case."

"Are you serious? Sam, that's horrible."

"No, what's horrible is that it took that damned ghost to give me the tips that let me figure it out. I've got to tell you that I'm getting kind of worried about your mother, she slipped into the Beauregard personality twice today and called me. I'm beginning to think it might be time for her to see a psychiatrist."

19

"You want to think that through," Indie said. "I mean, assuming she's crazy and Beauregard is just her own ability to predict the future, do you really want her to be cured? How many times has Beauregard saved your life now?"

"Shut up, I don't want to think about that right now. I just passed Belleview, how far ahead?"

"Um, it looks like about three quarters of a mile, and she's slowing down. The next major intersection is Bowles Avenue, or Littleton if she turns left. I'm watching, I'll let you know."

This section of 85 had more side streets, so Sam stood on his brakes and downshifted in order to slow down. He dropped down to just over eighty miles an hour, weaving through traffic and dodging emerging drivers. The Corvette handled it all like it was on a Sunday drive on an oval track.

"Sam, she's turning right onto Bowles Avenue. She's stopped at the moment, and I know that light, it's a long one. Be careful, but you might come up on her before she gets away from the intersection."

"I'll be careful," Sam said. "Once I get there, all I have to do is figure out which car she's in. Anything you can do to help me with that?"

"Yes, I can! There's another major intersection when she gets to Federal Boulevard, and it's got traffic cams. I can be hacked into them in a matter of seconds."

Sam could hear her tapping on the keyboard as he continued racing down the street. He could just see the intersection with Bowles Avenue up ahead of him when she spoke again. "Okay, I've got the cameras. She's coming up to the intersection in just a minute, and I should be able to tell which car she's in. Hang on, I'm watching."

"I'm hangin', babe," Sam said. He had downshifted in order to slow the car from its terrific speed, pumping the brakes to keep from overheating them. He was coming up fast on the intersection, and got the car under control in time to move into the right turn lane.

"Sam, it's one of two cars, but I can't get a look at the driver of either one to see if it's a woman. There's a big white car, almost looks like a police car without the lights, and right behind that is a black sports car, I think it's one of the new Corvettes."

The light was red for Sam, but he was still moving at

nearly 50 miles an hour as he came around the intersection. A couple of cars squealed their brakes as he slid in front of them, but then the Corvette straightened out and he floored it again. "Okay, babe, I'm about thirty seconds behind them. Let me take it from here, I've got to concentrate on driving."

"Okay, Sam, but you better call me as soon as you can. I'm gonna be worried sick, you know."

"I will, I will," Sam said. "Call Karen, let her know what's going on." A second later he heard the beep that said Indie had hung up.

The Federal Boulevard intersection loomed ahead, its light green, and Sam held the throttle to the floor. He was back up to a hundred and twenty and had no intention of losing speed, so he said a silent prayer and barreled ahead. The light turned yellow while he was still two hundred yards away, and he knew there was no hope of stopping.

Two cars started to enter the intersection of Federal, but Sam laid on his horn and both screeched to a stop as he shot through in front of them. There was another flurry of car horns and hand gestures, but Sam didn't even notice. He could see the two cars Indie described up ahead, and he was gaining on them rapidly.

Suddenly, the black Corvette whipped out and passed the car ahead of it, gaining speed like a rocket. "There you are!" Sam yelled. He had been about to slow down, but he pushed the throttle back to the floor and gave the old hot rod all it had.

There was no doubt in his mind that Jackie was driving the Z06 up ahead, and he knew that she had an incredible machine. The Z06 boasted six hundred and fifty horsepower, and was capable of speeds of two hundred and eighty-five miles per hour. It had been designed for road racing, and Sam's old 72 Stingray didn't have a tenth of the technological innovations that had gone into its design and production.

Sam didn't let that worry him. What his car did have was a high-compression 427 that had been a proven street dominator for decades. Sam had built the engine himself, spending more than twenty thousand dollars on the parts and accessories that made it as powerful as it could possibly be without being illegal. Since the road was leading through a massive residential area, there was very little chance that Jackie could get up to the monstrous speeds her car was capable of, so Sam knew he could keep up.

He grabbed his phone out of his pocket and quickly punched up Karen's number on speed dial. "I've got her," he yelled when she answered. "She's in a new black Corvette, doing about a hundred and forty miles an hour on Bowles Avenue, going west. I'm right behind her, keeping her in sight."

"Yeah, Indie told me. I hope you know we got phones going crazy down here about some idiots racing through that area. There's a half-dozen units already headed your way. You should be coming up on a roadblock shortly, Sam, so be careful."

Sam dropped his phone back into his pocket and concentrated on driving. Jackie was trying to shake him, weaving in and out of the traffic that was all over the road, but he was hanging on like a bulldog. They had gone about five miles when Jackie suddenly began to slow.

Sam had to downshift and ride his brakes to keep from crawling up her tailpipe, but then she whipped the car left on to Coal Mine Road. Sam followed, fishtailing around the corner and shifting like mad in order to get moving again. This road, however, was no straightaway. The long curve should have been a breeze for the Z06, but Sam could tell that Jackie was having trouble controlling the car.

His own Stingray, on the other hand, was a road-holding monster. He quickly found himself gaining on her again, and when she tried once more to get a burst of speed out of the car, he knew that she was going to lose control.

Sure enough, the Z06 went into a spin and left the road just past the Easton Sports Complex. A large empty field on the right suddenly became a massive cloud of dust as the car spun round and round. Sam slammed on his brakes and managed to bring his own car almost to a stop, then turned onto the dirt to follow Jackie.

The cloud of dust had kept him from seeing exactly

what happened, and when he found the Z06 he was shocked. Somewhere in that cloud, the car had dug in and begun flipping. Pieces of it were scattered over a half-acre, and he suddenly realized that what looked like a pile of rags in front of him was Jackie, herself.

Sam jumped out of the car and moved as quickly as he could to get to her, certain that there was no hope. Her body was mangled and broken, and blood was coming from various places, but when he dropped to his knees beside her she opened her eyes.

"Guess I really messed it up, didn't I, Sam?" Jackie said.

Sam yanked out his phone and dialed 911, but sirens were converging on him even as he told the dispatcher where to send an ambulance. A half-dozen squad cars skidded in around them, and several officers leaped out with their weapons drawn. Sam identified himself, and the officers hurried up to surround him and his suspect.

"Jackie, what in the world got into you?" Sam asked. "I know you killed McAlester, and you tried to kill the Howdens, but why?"

Jackie coughed, and a bit of blood spurted out of her mouth. "Got tired of him, I guess," she said. "I wasn't always bad, Sam, but do you know how hard it is for a tall girl to get a date? Carlos–he made me feel good, at first. He treated me good, and I liked it." She coughed again. "But then he started asking for favors, little things like making sure some small piece of evidence didn't make it to where it was supposed to be. At first I was scared, and just did it because I was afraid I'd lose him, but then it got to be kind of a game. I was outsmarting everyone, and that felt good." She started coughing once more, and it took her a few seconds to get it under control. "It all just went downhill, after that. You know what they say, the bigger the thrill you get, the bigger the one you need. Things just got completely out of hand, and I figured the only hope I had was to get him out of my life. I had it all planned out, so no one would get hurt but him; I didn't even know his ex was there until I got there that morning, and I thought the kid was at his grandparents. I slipped in the back, while they were yelling at each other, and I decided to go through with it when I heard her storm out the front door. I grabbed the knife and started toward the front, but then he turned around. When he saw me coming at him, he started to tell me to leave, that she would be back, but I couldn't stop myself. I already had the knife, and I just went a little crazy on him. As soon as he was down, I turned around and got out of there."

She took a ragged breath and Sam thought she was done, but she held on. Her eyes darted around at the officers surrounding her, and Sam wondered how many of them she knew.

"Jackie," Sam said, "he wasn't your first victim, was he?"

She turned her eyes back toward his face. "No. Like I said, the bigger the thrill...It grew, it grew like a monster that was out of control. First I was just losing little bits of evidence, then it was a matter of altering it. Before long, I was figuring out how to create evidence that would point the way Carlos wanted an investigation to go." She coughed again. "Then, one day, there was a witness, some guy who had seen something he wasn't supposed to see, but then he was in a wreck, and he got hurt. He was in the hospital, and Carlos was freaking out because if he talked, it would screw up whatever he was working on. He wanted me to fix it so no matter what the guy said, there wouldn't be any way to back it up, but I couldn't find a way to do that. Then it hit me it would just be better if the guy never said anything, and that seemed like the biggest thrill of all. I went to see him, and just added a bit more morphine to his IV."

Sam shook his head. "How many cases did you tamper with, Jackie?"

She rolled her eyes up to look into his own, and tried to shrug her shoulders. She suddenly grimaced in pain, and her breath started becoming more ragged.

"Too many..." Jackie gasped again, and then her eyes rolled up in her head. She was still breathing, but Sam didn't know if there was any hope or not.

He stayed there beside her until they heard the siren of the ambulance approaching, and when it slid in beside them, he got up and moved over to his car. Karen drove up just behind the ambulance, and walked over to where Sam was sitting on the fender of his Corvette.

"I don't know whether to pat you on the back or arrest you," Karen said. "In case you didn't notice, Sam, your car is not an authorized pursuit vehicle."

"Yeah, I know it," he said. "I couldn't let her get away, Karen. Chalk it up to me doing what I felt I had to do, and you can arrest me when you feel like it."

She snorted. "I'm not going to arrest you, and you know it." She looked over to where the paramedics were trying to stabilize Jackie enough to get her onto the stretcher. "You talk to her?"

"Yeah," Sam said, nodding. "After that kind of a wreck, I'm surprised she was alive, let alone conscious, but I talked to her. Apparently Carlos had gotten to her romantically, then when she was hooked, he started asking her for favors. Little things at first, I guess, tampering with evidence, but she said that it started to become a thrill for her to outsmart all of us, and she needed the thrills to be bigger. That eventually led her to murder, confirming the things I was told about her having killed before, but I'm not sure. She killed Carlos because she wanted out, wanted to quit."

Karen shook her head. "Just goes to show, doesn't matter how good we think we are, there's always some kind of temptation that can take us down the wrong path. Think she'll make it?"

"Hell, I ain't no doctor. If you asked me, I'd say she should have been dead ten minutes ago. If she makes it, maybe we can find out more about the things she did. If not, then I guess somebody's going to be going over all her crime scene and evidence reports for the last five years or more. Maybe when we know what cases she rigged, we'll start to get an idea of just how dark she went."

Karen stood there silently, watching with Sam as the paramedics finally got Jackie onto a backboard and into the ambulance. It rolled away quickly, its siren wailing once again.

"Well, I guess that's my cue," Karen said. "I'd better go down to the hospital and wait to see if she's got a chance. For her sake, it might be better if she didn't make it." She sighed dramatically. "At least she was single, that's one good thing."

Sam shrugged. "Was it? That's how Carlos got to her, that's how men like him always get to a woman, playing on her loneliness."

Karen looked at him for a moment. "Everyone is lonely, Sam, at least to some degree. All I really meant was that at least she wasn't leaving any kids behind. I worry every day about what would happen to mine if I got myself killed on the job." She shrugged her shoulders, then turned and walked away without another word.

20

Sam watched her go, then got into his car and fired it up to follow her to the hospital. It was certain that Jackie would be in surgery for some time, if she managed to pull through at all, but there were still questions that needed answers. Some of those he could get by hanging around Karen, but some would become unsolved mysteries if Jackie were to die.

"We might as well both go do something else," Karen said when he found her in the ER. "Doctor Klockenbrink told me to get the hell out of his way. He thinks she'll make it, but it will probably take several hours of surgery, and she won't be able to answer questions for at least a day."

Sam nodded. "I know she's in pretty bad shape," he said. "What about her CSI partner, Ned? Anybody figure out whether he was involved?"

"Couple of uniforms found him just a little bit ago,

back at work. He claims Jackie called him asking for a ride, said her car broke down. The way he tells it, he picked her up about three blocks from the Howdens' place, and she had him take her to the Chevy dealership where she stole the car she crashed. He claims he didn't even know there was a problem until they snatched him up and brought him downtown for questioning."

Sam grimaced and rolled his eyes. "He could be telling the truth," he said. "If Jackie was doing it for the thrills, it's doubtful she would've wanted to share them with anyone else. Besides, if she brought him in on it all, it would create the risk of a witness against her. I think if he knew what she was up to, he'd probably be dead already."

"Good point," Karen replied. "We'll give him the benefit of the doubt for now, unless we find evidence to the contrary. By the way, they're calling out Jack McGinty to run the crime lab for a while, and I guess he'll be handling all the case reviews. Unless we can find a particular point where her cases began getting skewed, he's going to have to go through every case she ever worked. Do you have any idea how many people could end up being released from prison because of this? How many cases that we thought were solved might be overturned?"

"Yeah, but there's an upside, too. Think of how many cases she tampered with so that we couldn't solve them. Going over the evidence with a fresh set of eyes might mean some of those will finally be closed."

Karen glared at him. "Oh, yeah, I forgot, you're an optimist. Just remember, buddy, you're not the one who's going to have to crawl all over those cold cases. At least some of them are going to fall in my lap."

Sam started to answer, but his phone rang. He glanced at it and saw that it was a call from Chris. "Gotta take this," he said to Karen, and then he walked away a few feet. "Hello?"

"Sam! Sam, you did it!" It wasn't Chris's voice that was screaming through the phone, but Candy's. "I'm out of jail, and guess what?"

Sam held the phone away from his ear. "What?"

"My lawyer, when he found out everything was being dismissed, he called CPS and started reading them the riot act. They're going to let me have Charlie, temporarily for right now, but we'll go to a permanent custody hearing in a few weeks. Isn't that awesome?"

Sam chuckled. "Yes, it sure is," he said. "Tell Charlie I said hello. That's a great kid you got there, Candy. I'm sorry things had to go this far south for you to get custody of him back, but I think it will be good for both of you to be together. When do you pick him up?"

"We're on the way to get him right now; he's at a group foster home in Littleton. Hey, Chris wants to talk to you." There was a moment of unidentifiable noise, then Chris came on the line.

"Sam, buddy, you're awesome! I knew if anybody could prove Candy innocent, you could. Let me know how much I owe you, I'm more than happy to pay."

"I'm not gonna send you a bill," Sam said. "We have to take care of our own, right? Let's just chalk this one up to doing what needed to be done."

"Well, like I said, you are definitely awesome. Anytime you need a favor in return, all you have to do is say the word. And I think that goes for all of us," Chris said, and Sam could hear Candy's heartfelt agreement in the background.

It took a minute or two for Sam to get off the phone, and by then, Karen was nowhere in sight. Sam wandered over to the information desk and found out that Mr. and Mrs. Howden had been admitted, got their room number and went to peek in on them. He found them on the third floor, sharing a room, and knocked lightly on the doorjamb.

Mrs. Howden was awake and sitting up in her bed, and she broke out into a big smile when she saw him. "Oh, come in, young man, come in," she said. "My husband tells me we have you to thank for our rescue."

Sam grinned at her. "I think we're even," he said. "I came to thank both of you for helping me solve the murder. You guys doing okay?"

"Oh, goodness, yes," the old woman said. "I'm a lot tougher than that silly girl imagined. I think she had some idea of trying to make it look like an accident, like a flowerpot was on an upper shelf and just fell on me. I don't know what she was planning to do to Kenneth, but it seems to me it would have looked pretty funny if we both died accidentally on the same day, don't you think?"

Sam had to stifle a chuckle. "Yes, that might have seemed a little bit odd. Luckily, I happened to stop by and interrupted her. When I found your husband, the only thing he could think about was trying to tell me where you were."

Mrs. Howden's eyebrows went up. "Really? That scamp," she said. "He should have been worried about himself, he was hurt a lot worse than I was. That crazy woman broke two of his ribs."

"Genevieve, I told you," Mr. Howden said, "my ribs are not broke. They're just bruised. All she did was push me down onto the bed, but I twisted my knee and couldn't get back up. If it hadn't been for that, I would have been right behind her with my Louisville slugger! Lucky for us this young feller showed up when he did." He turned to Sam. "Did you catch her?"

Sam gave him a half smile. "We got her, but I think she actually caught herself. I had found her on the street, and she decided to make a run for it. I was chasing her and she lost control of her car, rolled over several times. She's in surgery right now, but it looks like she might survive. Maybe then we can get to the bottom of this whole mess."

"What I don't understand is why she would have killed Carlos?" Mrs. Howden asked. "He was just the sweetest man you could ever have known."

"I'm afraid not everyone would agree with you on that, Mrs. Howden. It turns out that Carlos worked for a man who paid him to threaten and sometimes hurt people, just to make sure they did what he wanted them to do. Jackie—that's the lady who attacked you—she works for the police as a crime scene technician. I guess the two of them had a romantic relationship, her and Carlos, and he got her involved in his illegal activities. It seems she was trying to get out of it, and thought the only way she could do that was if Carlos was dead. She knew that if he was murdered, she'd be the one they called in to investigate the crime scene, and she could make the evidence look however she wanted. She just hadn't counted on me being hired to prove the number one suspect was innocent."

The old woman nodded wisely. "So she came after us because of the things we told you, right?"

"That's how I see it," Sam said. "I'm curious, though, why you never mentioned her as one of Carlos's girlfriends. I mean, you had to have seen her when she was going over the crime scene right across the street from you."

"I noticed that she was pretty tall, but I didn't realize it was the same tall girl I had seen going in there before. That one always wore a hood whenever she came over, and she drove a fancy blue car. I wish I would've known it was her, I could have probably saved us all a lot of trouble."

"Or you might have got us hurt a lot quicker," her husband said. "I told you all along, your nosiness was going to get us into trouble sooner or later, and it did."

Sam chuckled, and decided that was a good time for him to make his exit. He walked out of the room and took the elevator down to the main floor, then went out through the ER to get to where he had parked his car.

When he got to it, Sam paused for a moment to think about all that had happened over the past few days. Candy was free, and would soon be reunited with her son permanently. Jackie, who would probably go down for multiple murders and dozens of other crimes, was in surgery but expected to survive. The elderly couple who had helped Sam solve the case were going to be all right.

And Beauregard's track record was intact. Once again, he had been right.

Sam sat on the fender of his Corvette as he thought about all of these things, and then he took out his cell phone and called Indie.

"Hey, babe," he said. "You girls ready for me to come and join you?"

BOOK 10

COMING SOON!

Check Availability At:

WWW.DAVIDARCHER BOOKS.COM

ABOUT

David Archer was born and raised in Bakersfield, California. He is a fiction author and novelist, writing in the mysteries and thrillers genre. His approach to writing is to hit deep, keep you entertained, and leave you wanting MORE with every turn of the page. He writes mysteries, thrillers, and suspense novels, all of which are primed to get your heart pumping.

The author's books are a mixture of mystery, action, suspense, and humor. If you're looking for a good place to start, take a look at his bestselling Sam Prichard Novels, available now. You can grab copies in eBook, Audio, or Paperback on all major retailers.

Made in the USA
Coppell, TX
28 December 2020